ULTIMATE CROSSWORD PUZZLES

ULTIMATE CROSSWORD PUZZLES

From Easy to Tough

RUPA

Published by
Rupa Publications India Pvt. Ltd 2019
7/16, Ansari Road, Daryaganj
New Delhi 110002

Sales Centres:
Allahabad Bengaluru Chennai
Hyderabad Jaipur Kathmandu
Kolkata Mumbai

ISBN: 978-93-5333-576-2

First impression 2019

10 9 8 7 6 5 4 3 2 1

The moral right of the author has been asserted.

Introduction

In 1925, in the British magazine *Punch*, a cartoon was published about a man who phones his doctor in the middle of night asking for 'the name of a bodily disorder of seven letters, of which the second letter must be "N".' This cartoon said it all about the Crossword Mania.

You know the word, but it won't come to you. It lingers at the tip of your tongue. The moment you feel you have given up and you move on to the next clue, the elusive word appears right in front of you. You can actually never give up on a Crossword puzzle.

The first crosswords appeared in England during the nineteenth century. They were of an elementary kind, apparently derived from the word square, a group of words arranged so the letters read alike vertically and horizontally, and printed in children's puzzle books and various periodicals. In the United States, however, the puzzle developed into a serious adult pastime. The first modern crossword puzzle was published on 21 December 1913, in the New York World's Sunday supplement, *Fun*. It appeared as only one of a varied group of mental exercises, but it struck the fancy of the public. By 1923, crosswords were being published in most of the leading American newspapers, and the craze soon reached England. Soon, almost all daily newspapers in the United States and Great Britain had a crossword feature of some kind. *The Sunday Times* of London ran perhaps the best-known puzzle.

We have compiled in this volume a fancy collection of Crossword puzzles, which range from easy to difficult and, at times, very challenging. These are meant to entice you, challenge your mind and help you stay away from that smartphone!

And, as they say, the agony and the ecstasy of solving a crossword puzzle can reflect a surprising state of the subconscious mind.

We hope you will enjoy these puzzles as much as we have enjoyed curating them.

Quick crossword no 1

Across

1 Lithe (6)
4 Kind of tea (6)
9 Damage by speaking ill of (7)
10 The Surprise symphony composer, d. 1809 (5)
11 Unrehearsed (2,3)
12 Florence, for Italians (7)
13 Loosely woven cotton gauze (11)
18 Watership Down protagonists (7)
20 Until now (2,3)
22 Quavering note (5)
23 Person of no fixed abode (7)
24 Bible passage read as part of a church service (6)
25 Every seven days (6)

Down

1 Pedestrian tunnel (6)
2 Off-white colour (5)
3 Pleasant—genial (7)
5 Highly flammable liquid once used as an anaesthetic (5)
6 Type of light bulb fitting (7)
7 Hang around (6)
8 Harmless—not objectionable (11)
14 Leisure pursuits (7)
15 Baked pasta dish (7)
16 Hansel's sister (6)
17 Fairly—attractive (6)
19 Inuit abode (5)
21 Outspoken (5)

Quick crossword no 2

Across

1 Understood (12)
9 Musical composition with a theme repeated and developed (5)
10 Gun (7)
11 One of the Great Lakes (4)
12 European capital (8)
14 Unexpected and inexplicable change (6)
15 Commonly repeated word or phrase (6)
18 Marine mollusc (3,5)
20 Rebuff (4)
22 Bar—omit (7)
23 Freight (5)
24 Idle chatter (6-6)

Down

2 Currently in progress (7)
3 Writer of verse (4)
4 Strenuous exertion (6)
5 Centaurs (anag)—native of an ancient state of central Italy (8)
6 Cover loosely with a cloth (5)
7 11th-century land survey of England (8,4)
8 Fizzy (12)
13 Serene (8)
16 Clinging part of a plant (7)
17 Credit (anag)—steer (6)
19 Racecourse, home to the Gold Cup since 1807 (5)
21 Deer's tail (4)

Solution no 1

Quick crossword no 3

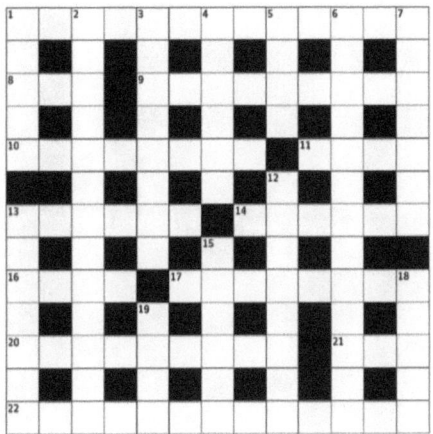

Across

1 Lovers' words? (5,8)
8 Nonsense (3)
9 Sneak out (5,4)
10 Flight recorder (5,3)
11 Unwilling (4)
13 Mother (or father) (6)
14 Hammered (6)
16 Without much rainfall (4)
17 Given as a gift (8)
20 Psychologically painful (9)
21 Commander of the Confederate States Army in the American Civil War (3)
22 Code breaking (13)

Down

1 Wash vigorously (5)
2 Remarkable (13)
3 Uzbek city on the old Silk Road (8)
4 Titania's king (6)
5 Assistance (4)
6 Australian state (3,5,5)
7 Words from the pourer? (3,4)
12 Upright (8)
13 Credit cards (7)
15 "Buster" of the silent films (6)
18 Garb (5)
19 Filth (4)

Solution no 2

Quick crossword no 4

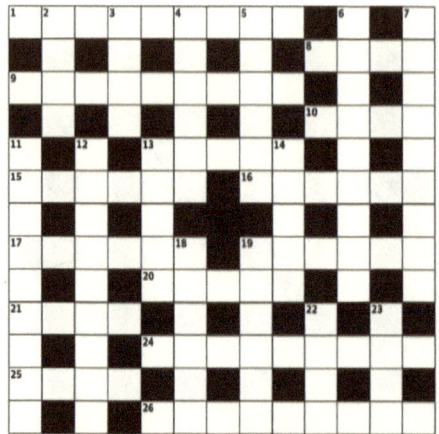

Across

1 Controversial issue (3,6)
8 Fish, often tinned (4)
9 Professional first names of Ferdinand Joseph LaMenthe Morton, d. 1941 (5,4)
10 Former Italian currency (4)
13 Small hill (5)
15 Seller (6)
16 What follows (6)
17 In actual fact (6)
19 Arabic salutation (6)
20 Goddess (5)
21 Duty list (4)
24 Go too far (9)
25 Volition (4)
26 Every second one (9)

Down

2 Kitchen appliance (4)
3 Arrange in stacks (4)
4 Lethargy (6)
5 Sharply hooked claws (6)
6 Cable railway (9)
7 Tibetan religious leader (5,4)

11 In the red (9)
12 Childish (9)
13 Furry growth of minute fungi (5)
14 Hold-up (5)
18 Somerset town on the Fosse Way (6)
19 Deprive of food (6)
22 Slender (4)
23 The majority (4)

Solution no 3

Quick crossword no 5

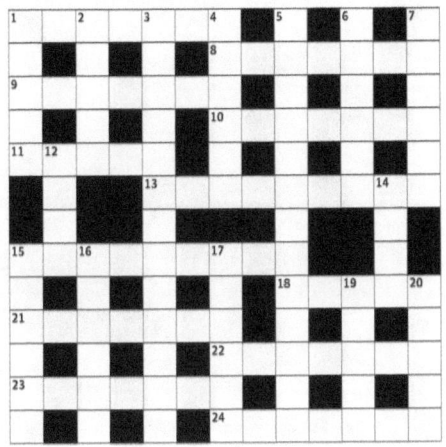

Across

1 Flower (7)
8 Expressing love (7)
9 One who speaks excessively (7)
10 Nasal aperture (7)
11 Sloping mass of loose rock (5)
13 Rest (9)
15 Intermediary (2-7)
18 Trials—tribulations (5)
21 Offensive remarks (7)
22 Shopping container (7)
23 (Of pasta) firm when eaten (2,5)
24 Slices of bacon (7)

14 Compass point (4)
15 Six-stringed instrument (6)
16 Compared with (6)
17 Festival after Lent (6)
19 Balm—ointment (5)
20 Eye infections (5)

Down

1 Game on a green (5)
2 Proprietor (5)
3 Aggressive display of military force (5-8)
4 Large bottle (6)
5 Painstaking (13)
6 Very unpleasant (6)
7 Old stableman at an inn—sterol (anag) (6)
12 Small north Pacific salmon (4)

Solution no 4

Quick crossword no 6

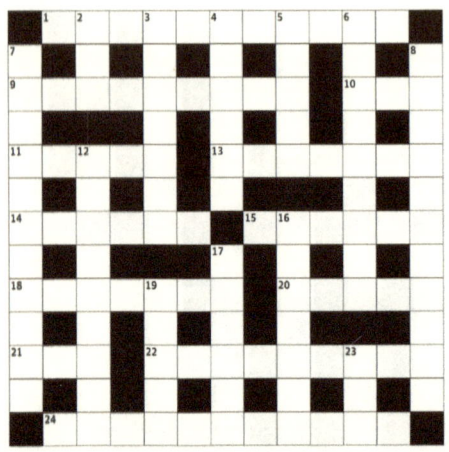

Across

1 Remain south (anag)—migratory bird (5,6)
9 Forerunner (9)
10 Sound made by a pigeon (3)
11 Dusk to dawn (5)
13 Purported (7)
14 Hostelry (6)
15 Pounce—pogo stick part (6)
18 Meander (anag) (7)
20 Drink alcohol (5)
21 Not many (3)
22 Shopping by post (4,5)
24 Striking (3-8)

17 Junkie (6)
19 Ape (5)
23 Loud noise (3)

Down

2 Half and half? (3)
3 Stroll (7)
4 Foreign intelligence agency (6)
5 Relating to the countryside (5)
6 With one's identity concealed (9)
7 Wastrel (11)
8 Fictitious name (3,2,6)
12 Yielding (6,3)
16 Bagpipe music (7)

Solution no 5

Quick crossword no 7

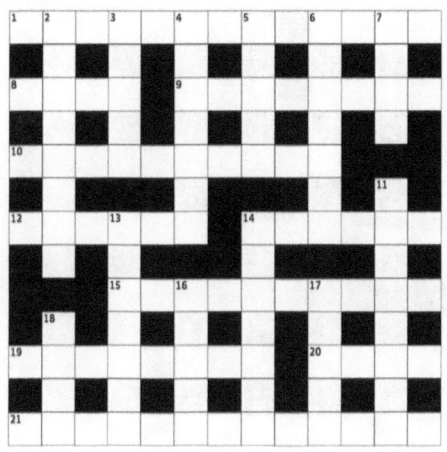

Across

1 Blameless—totally honest (5,8)
8 Mark left by a wound (4)
9 Like new (8)
10 Large fly—wild cornflower (10)
12 Maintain formally (6)
14 Alkali-metal element, Na (6)
15 Richer post (anag)—top administrative position in some universities and colleges (10)
19 Writer of words set to music (8)
20 Flower—girl's name (4)
21 Causing great distress (13)

17 Self-satisfied smile (5)
18 Unit of (usually eight) bits (4)

Down

2 Strong negative reaction (8)
3 Edge (5)
4 Harmonious relationship (7)
5 Significance (5)
6 Very fashionable (2-5)
7 Edible ice cream container (4)
11 Trial performance for an artiste (8)
13 Before now (7)
14 Breed of terrier (7)
16 Ascent (5)

Solution no 6

Quick crossword no 8

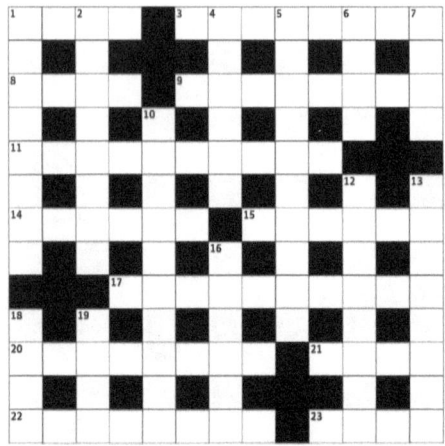

Across

1 Karate blow (4)
3 Draughts in America (8)
8 Bottle part (4)
9 Scottish North Sea city (8)
11 Compulsive purchaser (10)
14 Very (4,2)
15 Conforming to Jewish dietary law (6)
17 One lost bet (anag)—kind of whale or dolphin (10)
20 Sound made by a mobile phone (8)
21 Kerfuffle (2-2)
22 Imaginary evil spirit, used to frighten children (8)
23 Horse-breeding establishment (4)

Down

1 Storage container (8)
2 Cursory examination (4-4)
4 Hang out with people of standing (6)
5 Meat-eaters (10)
6 Regards—features of a potato (4)
7 Hourglass contents (4)
10 Author of The Forsyte Saga (10)
12 Gunfight (5-3)

13 Permanent tenure of land or property (8)
16 Lines forming a unit of verse (6)
18 Seize—snatch (4)
19 Indulge in amorous activity (4)

Solution no 7

Quick crossword no 9

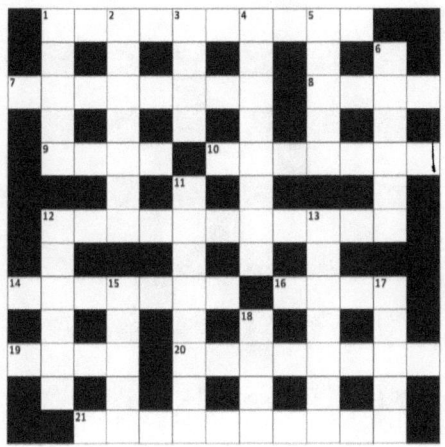

Across

1 Contrived (10)
7 Something made out of a molehill? (8)
8 Furnished holiday house in France (4)
9 Gardener's basket (4)
10 Espied (7)
12 Old county of north-west England (11)
14 Area with fruit trees (7)
16 Run smoothly (4)
19 Lacking sparkle (4)
20 Wizard (8)
21 On the face of it (10)

12 In a cautious manner (6)
13 Malady (7)
15 Angry—agitated (3,2)
17 Tearful (5)
18 Unencumbered (4)

Down

1 To great height (5)
2 Languages (7)
3 Anti-aircraft fire (4)
4 Plot (8)
5 Acute, but unspecific, feeling of anxiety (5)
6 Be present (6)
11 Food of the gods (8)

Solution no 8

Quick crossword no 10

Across

1 Agreement ending a dispute (10)
7 Type of lettuce (7)
8 Drinking chocolate (5)
10 Piece of legislation—one of the Clintons (4)
11 Quadruple (8)
13 Too (6)
15 Emphasis (6)
17 Public open space in Central London (4,4)
18 Attempt (4)
21 Less often seen (5)
22 Old saw (7)
23 Almost without hope (10)

Down

1 Period of time (5)
2 Ash, for example (4)
3 Body of salt water cut off from the sea (6)
4 Cream tea (anag)—soften by steeping in liquid (8)
5 Congratulatory phrase (4,3)
6 1984's totalitarian controller—TV reality show (3,7)
9 African capital (5,5)
12 Balderdash (8)
14 Back (7)
16 Visit informally (4,2)
19 Short online message (5)
20 One of Hamlet's questionable options? (2,2)

Solution no 9

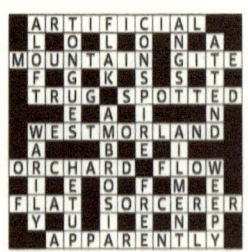

Quick crossword no 11

Across

1 Groups of connected pages on the World Wide Web (8)
5 Was contrite about (4)
9 Crave something belonging to someone else (5)
10 Measure of noise intensity (7)
11 Hair styling device (7,5)
13 Geometrician of the 3rd century BC (6)
14 Japanese religion (6)
17 Corrupt males (anag)—French author (6,6)
20 Diminished (7)
21 Ingenuous (5)
22 Male deer (4)
23 Members of a male religious order (8)

Down

1 Texas city linked to a 1993 siege and massacre (4)
2 Camp out (7)
3 Brains—news (12)
4 Termination (6)
6 Relating to a densely populated area (5)
7 Erroneous belief (8)
8 Hot chilli pepper—connects both (anag) (6,6)
12 Sully (8)
15 More unpleasant (7)
16 Eight-legged creature (6)
18 Electronic detection system (5)
19 Average (4)

Solution no 10

Quick crossword no 12

Across

1 Ballet dancer's skirt (4)
3 Using bad language (8)
9 Strong wind down the 20 valley (7)
10 Robinson Crusoe author (5)
11 Senior member of a group (5)
12 Despot (6)
14 I'm a notable nut (anag)—Cape Town feature (5,8)
17 Being nosy (6)
19 Rapidly becoming popular online (5)
22 Regions (5)
23 Tiresome (7)
24 Removed—mimicked (5,3)
25 Contradict (4)

Down

1 Lack of assertiveness (8)
2 Irritable (5)
4 Esteemed (4,7,2)
5 Snake (like an abacus?) (5)
6 Spanish princess (7)
7 Scottish valley (4)
8 (Get a) tan (6)
13 British island known locally as Ynys Môn (8)
15 In a violent frenzy (7)
16 South-west US state (6)
18 Norwegian dramatist (5)
20 River running from the Swiss Alps to the Mediterranean (5)
21 Abstain from eating (4)

Solution no 11

Quick crossword no 13

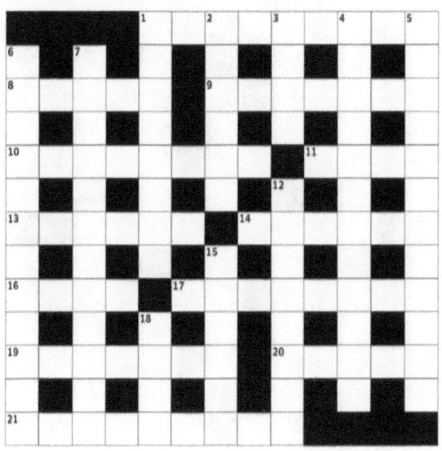

Across

1 Beast of burden (9)
8 Rejoice (5)
9 Shortfall (7)
10 More than anything else (5,3)
11 Tranquil (4)
13 French regional dialect (6)
14 Wanton destroyer (6)
16 Large number—killed (4)
17 Agnostic (anag)—moving easily (8)
19 Country on the Red Sea (7)
20 Chess pieces (5)
21 Spend money freely (6,3)

12 Ancient official language of India (8)
15 Spud (6)
18 Greek god of war (4)

Down

1 Hopelessly inadequate (8)
2 Pamper—cook in nearly boiling water (6)
3 Fit of irritation (4)
4 US vice president, 1953-61 and president, 1969–74 (7,5)
5 One who studies insects (12)
6 Cyclists—women's calf-length trousers (5,7)
7 Mediocre (3-2-3-4)

Solution no 12

Quick crossword no 14

Across

1 Bet—Procter's partner (6)
4 High-flyer in Greek mythology (6)
8 Stupefied (5)
9 Type of bet (4-3)
10 Explosive part of a missile (7)
11 Nip (5)
12 Increased (9)
17 Scope (5)
19 Fairly large (7)
21 Mounted soldiers (7)
22 Free (5)
23 Badmouth (6)
24 Flat steel tool with a cutting edge (6)

Down

1 Subside (2,4)
2 Polish folk dance (7)
3 Projecting ridge (5)
5 Pilot's compartment (7)
6 Mountain ash (5)
7 Old farming tool (6)
9 Ad infinitum (9)
13 Wild goose—eg gyral (anag) (7)
14 Doubtful (7)

15 Unit of apothecary weight (6)
16 Expose (6)
18 Belly button (5)
20 Diddly-squat (5)

Solution no 13

Quick crossword no 15

Across

5 Statements about the future (11)
7 Wee drop of whisky? (4)
8 Thin slice of boneless meat (8)
9 Bound by oath (7)
11 Striped quadruped (5)
13 Fishing vessel (5)
14 Dull—commonplace (7)
16 Sick headache (8)
17 Elegantly stylish (4)
18 Minced meat in pastry snack (7,4)

Down

1 Smile radiantly (4)
2 Magi (4,3)
3 Lodged (5)
4 Coal miners (8)
5 International competition for disabled athletes (11)
6 Far from thorough (11)
10 Seemly (8)
12 Felt great sorrow (7)
15 King with the golden touch (5)
17 Dog—food (4)

Solution no 14

Quick crossword no 16

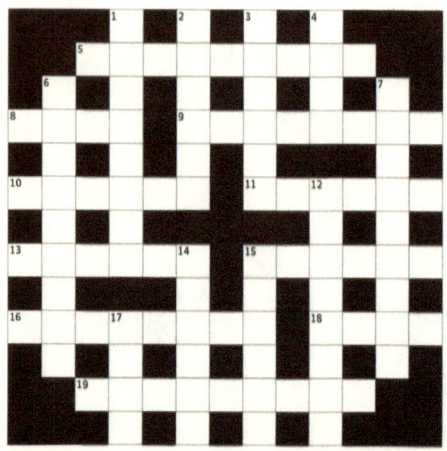

Across

5 Greek dramatist, author of Oedipus Rex (9)
8 Metal, Au (4)
9 Tire oneself out (6,2)
10 Mad (6)
11 Flat-topped pieces of furniture (which can be turned?) (6)
13 Sand trap (6)
15 US state, capital Salem (6)
16 Suffered anguish (8)
18 Food fish related to the cod (4)
19 Stolen (9)

14 Consequence (6)
15 South London theatre (3,3)
17 Substantive (4)

Down

1 Refrain—restrain—retain (4,4)
2 Protective finish on motor vehicle fittings (6)
3 Take—consent (6)
4 Flex (4)
6 Lunar rover (4,5)
7 Pyrotechnics (9)
12 President of the USSR, 1977-82 (8)

Solution no 15

Quick crossword no 17

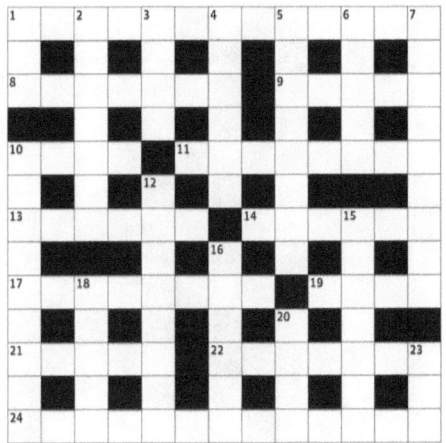

Across

1 Providing double security (4,3,6)
8 Farm vehicle (7)
9 Hold firmly (5)
10 Brewery product (4)
11 Rotary (8)
13 London rail terminus (6)
14 Deft (6)
17 Courgette (8)
19 South African currency (4)
21 Major's successor as PM (5)
22 Experienced sailors? (3,4)
24 Refrain from talking (6,4,3)

16 International agency—no cues (anag) (6)
18 Nautical map (5)
20 Hamlet was one (4)
23 Fluid in a plant (3)

Down

1 Binary digit (3)
2 Several (anag)—Brexiteers (7)
3 Play parts (4)
4 Author of The Descent of Man (6)
5 Killer of a king (8)
6 Go on all fours (5)
7 Distinguished—divided (9)
10 Prince of Darkness (9)
12 Philanderer (8)
15 Enjoying a winning streak (2,1,4)

Solution no 16

Quick crossword no 18

Across

1 Brilliancy (6)
4 Savour (5)
7 Fashion—style (6)
8 Bold as brass (6)
9 Muck (4)
10 Dreadful (8)
12 A cold manner (anag)—firework (5,6)
17 Binding agreement (8)
19 Wingless bloodsucking parasites (4)
20 Slightly drunk (6)
21 Antagonism (6)
22 Contented (5)
23 Frightened (6)

14 Quandary (7)
15 Worked up (7)
16 Whisky (6)
18 Mass meeting—revive (5)

Down

1 Having more foliage (7)
2 Sacred place (7)
3 Fictional central European kingdom (9)
4 Mistake (5)
5 Shameless painted woman (7)
6 Over there (6)
11 Traditional English food (5,4)
13 Confessed (5,2)

Solution no 17

Quick crossword no 19

Across

1 Uneven (6)
4 Group of words forming part of a sentence (6)
9 FT index—flirty under-the-table play (7)
10 Relax one's efforts (3,2)
11 River and department of southeast France (5)
12 Dictionary (7)
13 Dejected after a failure (11)
18 Nouveau riche (7)
20 Balance—composure (5)
22 Head monk (5)
23 Joyce novel (7)
24 Repeated prayers (6)
25 Chesty (anag)—tool (6)

Down

1 Seabird with a short neck and brightly coloured bill (6)
2 Treasure of unknown ownership (5)
3 Person providing hospitality (7)
5 Three-dimensional object shaped like a corkscrew (5)
6 Newscaster's reading aid (7)
7 Mushroom (6)
8 Sweet-sounding (11)
14 Arbiter (anag)—snack (7)
15 Linking of speaker's mouth movements and voice in filmed recordings (3,4)
16 Sit with one's limbs spread out (6)
17 Loch monster? (6)
19 Gobbled up (5)
21 Something put into something else (5)

Solution no 18

Quick crossword no 20

Across

1 Instruction on a hotel bedroom door? (2,3,7)
9 With toad-like blemishes (5)
10 Guidance (7)
11 Academy of Television Arts and Sciences award (4)
12 Current beneath breaking wave (8)
14 Malicious—licentious (6)
15 Fleshy bit of the buttocks (6)
18 Place of trials (3,5)
20 Thrash (4)
22 Woolly (7)
23 Online message (5)
24 Of a large city—London Underground line (12)

Down

2 Rower (7)
3 Long-horned African antelope (4)
4 Pour wine into another container (6)
5 Pot (8)
6 Unexpected result (5)
7 Unfair (5,3,4)
8 Garden pink—Willie wet Sam (anag) (5,7)
13 US state (with a beetle) (8)
16 Ultimate tranquil state (7)
17 Pretty cave (6)
19 Cereal grass (5)
21 Food shop (abbr) (4)

Solution no 19

Quick crossword no 21

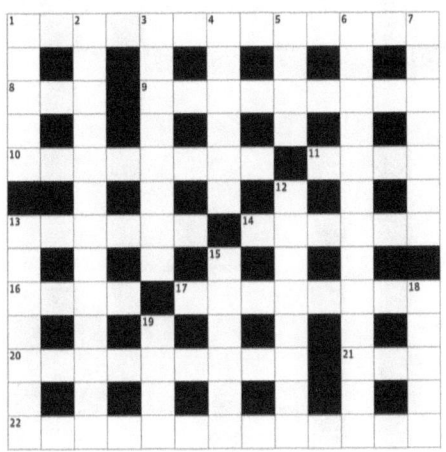

Across

1. Hanging item to protect a theatre audience (6,7)
8. Botham or Chappell? (3)
9. Government treasury department (9)
10. Hand-held firework (8)
11. Unit of heredity (4)
13. Sesame-seed based foodstuff (6)
14. Viz (6)
16. Style (4)
17. Furtive (8)
20. Mysterious items—ciao trees (anag) (9)
21. Point (3)
22. Tease (4,3,6)

Down

1. From Zurich, say? (5)
2. Type of cured fish (6,7)
3. Arduous walking (8)
4. Distinction (6)
5. Stink (4)
6. Funfair (9,4)
7. Where young plants grow up? (7)

12. Atomic bomb target, 9 August 1945 (8)
13. Violent disturbance (7)
15. Discord (6)
18. That tastes great! (5)
19. Infernal nuisance (4)

Solution no 20

Quick crossword no 22

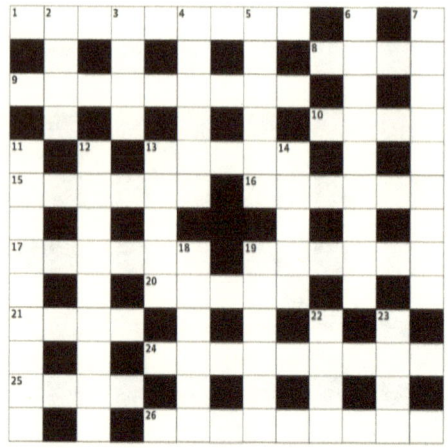

Across

1 Carry on the back and shoulders (9)
8 Stop—stalk (4)
9 Made to withstand serious wear (5-4)
10 Operatic vocal (4)
13 Ultimate (5)
15 Challenge (to be cleared) (6)
16 Long John Silver's Captain Flint (6)
17 Renowned (6)
19 Blind temporarily (6)
20 The Lone Star State (5)
21 Tiny bit (4)
24 Barbara Bush or Michelle Obama? (5,4)
25 Chewed shrub (4)
26 Something of little importance (5,4)

Down

2 Mountain goat (4)
3 Hand over (4)
4 Villain (6)
5 Quick snooze (6)
6 Impatient at having nothing to do (in prison?) (4,5)
7 Beset by difficulties (9)
11 Small songbird (9)
12 Chicken leg (9)
13 Treat with contempt (5)
14 Tibetan priests (5)
18 Discriminatory or abusive behaviour (6)
19 Maiden (often in distress) (6)
22 Soft globule (4)
23 Doing nothing (4)

Solution no 21

Quick crossword no 23

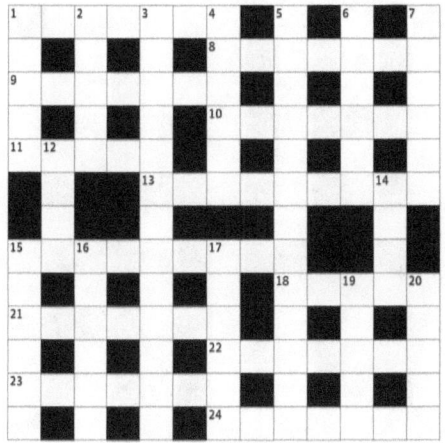

Across

1 Strip of land with water on both sides (7)
8 French castle (7)
9 Isolated—urinals (anag) (7)
10 Gases ejected from an engine (7)
11 Rapacious desire (5)
13 Completely full (3-6)
15 Person compelled to work for pay in order to survive (4,5)
18 One with very long sentence (5)
21 Smallest amount (7)
22 First (7)
23 Set up (7)
24 Effect where combined actions produce a greater effect than the sum of individual efforts (7)

Down

1 Cake topping (5)
2 Savour (5)
3 Inability to cope with a normal environment (13)
4 Person who seems extremely funny? (6)
5 Cunning and unscrupulous (13)
6 Show to be false (6)
7 Reduced to a shell (6)
12 Asian prince or king (4)
14 Effortlessness (4)
15 Marsupial of Oz (6)
16 Bridge-like overhead structure (6)
17 Hosts (6)
19 Religious order member (5)
20 Race with baton changes (5)

Solution no 22

Quick crossword no 24

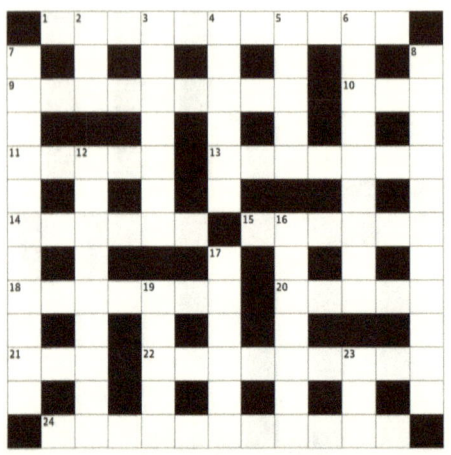

Across

1 Disagreement (11)
9 For ever (9)
10 Exclamation of surprise or pain (3)
11 Give birth (to an iceberg?) (5)
13 More courageous (7)
14 Hole (6)
15 In need of slapping down? (6)
18 Xylophone-like instrument from Africa (7)
20 In accordance with the law (abbr) (5)
21 Tough timber (3)
22 Amount taken away (9)
24 Ecstatic (2,5,4)

17 Four-wheeled horse-drawn carriage (6)
19 Gong (5)
23 Electrically charged particle (3)

Down

2 Mineral containing valuable metal (3)
3 Straight line just touching a curve (7)
4 Formally expressed praise (6)
5 Land of the lower Nile (5)
6 Favourable—hopeful (9)
7 Vagrant living by the sea (11)
8 Hard middle of a red fruit (6,5)
12 Member of a City Company (9)
16 Seabird with a large pouched bill (7)

Solution no 23

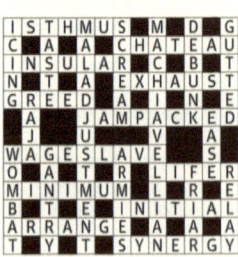

Quick crossword no 25

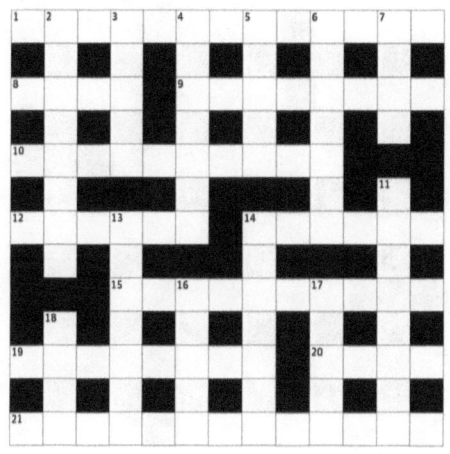

Across

1 Someone willing to trade favours for mutual advantage? (13)
8 Open pastry case (4)
9 Somewhat unreasonable or OTT (1,3,4)
10 Sleuth (10)
12 Source of danger (6)
14 Disturbance (6)
15 Urchin (10)
19 Unpredictable factor (4,4)
20 Skating jump with a turn (4)
21 Another item? (9,4)

Down

2 Signal that it's safe to come out (3,5)
3 Japanese martial art using split bamboo swords (5)
4 Was incompatible (7)
5 Bye (5)
6 Funny (7)
7 Per person (4)
11 Commercial activity (8)
13 Curtail (7)
14 Islam's holiest month (7)

16 Grind (one's teeth) (5)
17 Burner—passion (5)
18 Cylindrical storage tower (4)

Solution no 24

Quick crossword no 26

Across

1 Short, light breath of wind (4)
3 Nous (8)
8 Marching orders? (4)
9 Gritty (like some sugar?) (8)
11 Involving very poor social conditions—case in kind (anag) (10)
14 Mechanical force causing rotation (6)
15 Mexican cocktail made with white rum and lime juice (6)
17 Regardless (5-5)
20 Morning call (8)
21 Cain's younger brother (4)
22 The 'John' of 'John Smith' (8)
23 Summons (4)

Down

1 Assign to a later time (8)
2 Queen or Jack, say? (4,4)
4 Agitation (6)
5 Baggy trousers gathered at the ankles (10)
6 Ailments—misfortunes (4)
7 Informer (4)
10 Person giving hair and skin treatments etc (10)
12 Atmospheric pressure unit (8)
13 Speaker of many languages (8)
16 Downhill ski event (6)
18 High-ranking university academic (abbr) (4)
19 Six balls, as a unit (4)

Solution no 25

Quick crossword no 27

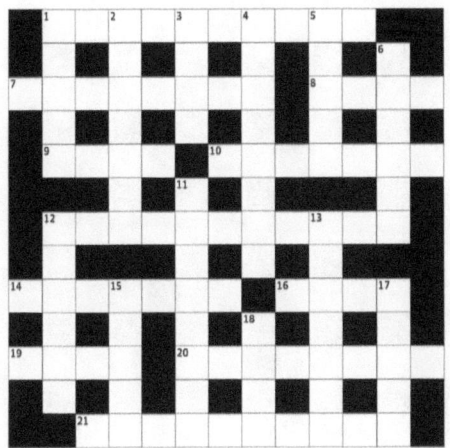

Across

1 Signal letter Q, flown to indicate ship is carrying disease (6,4)

7 Marsupial that boxes (8)

8 Ukrainian capital (4)

9 System of weights for measuring precious metals and gemstones (4)

10 Entertainment industry (7)

12 Hot and cold sweet (5,6)

14 Lethargy (7)

16 Truncheon (4)

19 Slovenly layabout (4)

20 Youngster (8)

21 Varied collection (10)

Down

1 Leavening agent (5)

2 Long and tedious effort involved in gathering basic information (7)

3 Gumbo (4)

4 Small area captured and held as the basis for subsequent advance (8)

5 Crooked (5)

6 Eye part (6)

11 Sea between Italy and the Balkans (8)

12 Mess up (6)

13 Dried pale yellow seedless grape (7)

15 Jewish teacher (5)

17 Athletic and muscular (nonvegetarian?) (5)

18 Longitudinal structure supporting the frame of a vessel (4)

Solution no 26

Quick crossword no 28

Across

1 Bavarian shorts with braces (10)
7 Candid (7)
8 North American plant with swordshaped leaves (5)
10 Coughs up (4)
11 Not in keeping with accepted standards (8)
13 Hurry (6)
15 Suddenly go berserk (4,2)
17 Lovely (8)
18 Imitate—a nymph (4)
21 Well known (5)
22 Put at risk (7)
23 Selfishly, just take the best bits (6-4)

12 Back (8)
14 Time period (7)
16 Provide with goods (6)
19 Make a sound like a hen (5)
20 (Person who is) not in favour (4)

Down

1 Tall (5)
2 Arab lateen-rigged sailing ship (4)
3 Score (6)
4 Contradictory figure of speech (8)
5 Small territory completely surrounded by another one (7)
6 Start too quickly (4,3,3)
9 Tried out for a part (10)

Solution no 27

Quick crossword no 29

Across

1 Hot breakfast food (8)
5 Smear (4)
9 Egyptian peninsula (5)
10 Rattle (7)
11 Daring and romantic adventurer (12)
13 Unspecified person (6)
14 Foot-operated boat (6)
17 Too informally clothed for the occasion (12)
20 Metal cutter (7)
21 Loud and rude (5)
22 Affectedly creative (4)
23 Stupid (8)

16 Gardener's tool (6)
18 Old gold coin (5)
19 Units of electrical resistance (4)

Down

1 Upper-class (4)
2 Absconder (7)
3 Foible (12)
4 Soiled (6)
6 Start of the financial year (5)
7 Purple vegetable (8)
8 Difficult to reach (12)
12 Elderly Russian woman (8)
15 Norm (7)

Solution no 28

Quick crossword no 30

Across

1 Part of ear or leaf (4)
3 Medical fitness examination (8)
9 Travelling show with rides, games and much else (7)
10 Parts to play (5)
11 Lolly (5)
12 Invulnerable (6)
14 Capacity to cause trouble (8,5)
17 Hindu deity, the Preserver (6)
19 Error (5)
22 Natural stream (5)
23 He loots (anag)—southern African kingdom (7)
24 Separate (8)
25 Professional cook (4)

Down

1 Socialist (4-4)
2 Old West African kingdom from which 'bronze' sculptures were looted by the British in 1897 (5)
4 Poetic form used by Chaucer—ochre poultice (anag) (6,7)
5 Amber-coloured fluid in the blood (5)
6 Army officer ranking below a brigadier (7)
7 Carnal desire (4)
8 Fruit (for a split?) (6)
13 Full moon howler (8)
15 Hostile or cold nature (7)
16 Small travelling bag (6)
18 One on a long walk (5)
20 Sewn-on piece of material (5)
21 Move quickly (as if running before a gale) (4)

Solution no 29

Quick crossword no 31

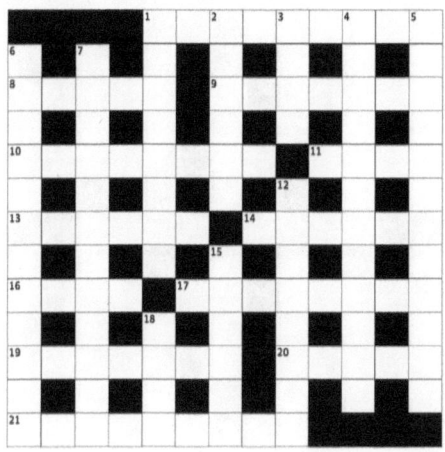

Across

1 Something beyond criticism (6,3)
8 Vietnamese capital (5)
9 Helper or attendant (sometimes humble or obedient?) (7)
10 Render motionless (8)
11 Emperor (4)
13 Short-sighted (6)
14 Old mercantile area of Venice (6)
16 Emperor (who fiddled while Rome burned?) d. AD68 (4)
17 Seed of a palm chewed (with its leaves) as a narcotic (5,3)
19 Judge (7)
20 Round Dutch cheese (5)
21 Pine, for example (9)

Down

1 Outfit for a dip (8)
2 Sweet blackcurrant liqueur (6)
3 Get by working (4)
4 Sofa for reclining on (6,6)
5 Carnivorous aquatic bug (5,7)
6 Composite picture (12)
7 Ominous—critical (12)

12 Professional killer (5,3)
15 Order (6)
18 Stockmarket operator gambling on a quick profit (4)

Solution no 30

Quick crossword no 32

Across

1 Poor handwriting (6)
4 Musical interval of 12 semitones (6)
8 Birthplace of the Prophet Mohammed (5)
9 Discordant (7)
10 Tiddly (7)
11 Heraldic device representing a family (5)
12 Coming from Taipei? (9)
17 Forelock brushed upward (5)
19 Red sauce (7)
21 Unpaid (7)
22 Holy Writ (5)
23 Thrill (6)
24 Storey (anag) (6)

9 Careless pedestrian (9)
13 Vary the voice pitch (7)
14 Something shown in public (7)
15 Stick-in-the-mud—quadrangle (6)
16 Seem (6)
18 Father of Jacob and Esau (5)
20 Cat with a mottled coat (5)

Down

1 Triangular Indian turnover (6)
2 Narrate in detail (7)
3 Waterfront landing stage (5)
5 Small round boat of hides stretched over a wicker frame (7)
6 Existent (5)
7 The latest Henry or Edward? (6)

Solution no 31

Quick crossword no 33

Across

5 Vodka and orange juice (11)
7 Highly excited (4)
8 Nonconformist (8)
9 Old ship—cooking utensil (7)
11 Intense nervous excitement or anticipation? (5)
13 Milky coffee (5)
14 Cut of beef from the breast or lower chest (7)
16 Swift's land of tiny people (8)
17 Sudden jerk (4)
18 Huge oil transporter (11)

17 Gag (4)

Down

1 Steep rugged rock (4)
2 Person moving through water (7)
3 Meat jus (5)
4 Abroad (8)
5 Heavenly archer (11)
6 Nelson__, Gerald Ford's vice president (11)
10 Springbok or gnu? (8)
12 Narrow-bladed cutter (7)
15 Flicker—provoke (5)

Solution no 32

Quick crossword no 34

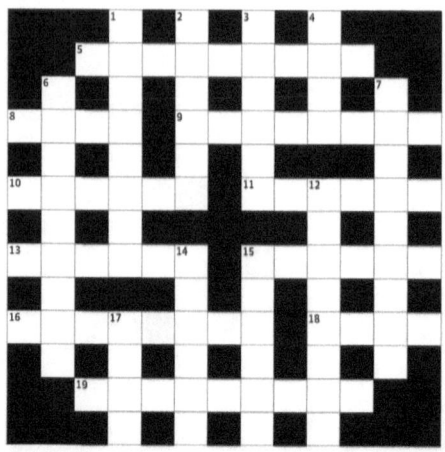

Across

5 Offer one's services (9)
8 Actor's departure (4)
9 Fishing gear that floats with the current (5,3)
10 Plane figure elongated in one direction (6)
11 Pea, bean or lentil? (6)
13 (Cause to) stumble (4,2)
15 To lope (anag)—move in a leisurely way (6)
16 Spectator (8)
18 Sheep coat (4)
19 Sincere (9)

15 Cleanse (6)
17 Domesticated bovines (4)

Down

1 (Use) flattering talk (4,4)
2 Retriever (3,3)
3 As you please (2,4)
4 Give free expression to—opening (4)
6 In high spirits (9)
7 Bright scarlet (9)
12 Feeling of generosity towards others (8)
14 Fire irons (6)

Solution no 33

Quick crossword no 35

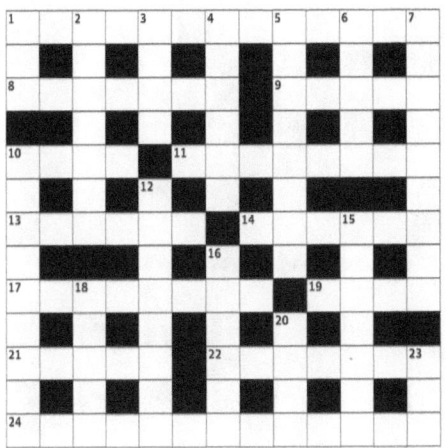

Across

1 Warehouse vehicle (4-4,5)
8 Snow White's self-consciously timid assistant (7)
9 First notes (5)
10 Nimble (4)
11 Respite and a cuppa (3,5)
13 Agile—quick (6)
14 Spiny shrub with clusters of yellow or white flowers (6)
17 Cistern floater (8)
19 Fine fabric—senior barrister (4)
21 Portend (5)
22 Wipe the floor with (7)
24 Phone selling and promotion (13)

Down

1 Lie (3)
2 Speaker's platform (7)
3 Raise (4)
4 Strain (6)
5 Queue of traffic (8)
6 Release (5)
7 Disappointing rejection (5-4)

10 Clean using a pressurised jet—salt bands (anag) (9)
12 Guitarist's aid (8)
15 Italian wine (7)
16 Large duck—corset (anag) (6)
18 Permissible (5)
20 Shoe part—lone (4)
23 Cooked breakfast staple (3)

Solution no 34

Quick crossword no 36

Across

1 Woman's shirt (6)

4 Noisy confusion of voices (5)

7 Line of fibres twisted to form a thread (6)

8 Rectangular array of mathematical data set out in rows and columns (6)

9 Desert of central China (4)

10 Division of an academic year (8)

12 Lather aiding beard removal (7,4)

17 With the press and public excluded (2,6)

19 One of a similar pair (4)

20 Armed robber (6)

21 Narcotic drug (6)

22 Herb used in cooking as seasoning (5)

23 Dash joining words (6)

Down

1 Baron Hardup's servant in Cinderella (7)

2 Egg-shaped wind instrument with finger holes (7)

3 Glancing blow (9)

4 Light-coloured marking on a horse's face (5)

5 Stiff cap worn by Roman Catholic clergy (7)

6 Extravagance (6)

11 Of birds that move seasonally (9)

13 Carriage for hire (7)

14 Largest living bird (7)

15 Wet (7)

16 Gallows (6)

18 Plant producing sweetcorn (5)

Solution no 35

Quick crossword no 37

Across

1 Look out (6)
4 Given a sweetener (6)
9 Keenly excited (7)
10 Chores (5)
11 Device producing an intense beam of light (5)
12 Had nice (anag)—spiny anteater (7)
13 Attract a great deal of attention (4,1,6)
18 Pilot (7)
20 Creator of Eeyore (5)
22 Spanish red wine (5)
23 Chilean desert (7)
24 Much obliged (6)
25 Stir up (6)

14 The Grand Canyon State (7)
15 Lower back ache (7)
16 Attic (6)
17 21 (6)
19 Pursue (5)
21 Time off (5)

Down

1 Small hound (6)
2 Collection of closely packed trees (5)
3 Book—store (7)
5 Strain, as if to vomit (5)
6 As well as (7)
7 Deprive of the rights of a barrister (6)
8 Combative (11)

Solution no 36

Quick crossword no 38

Across

1 Malinger—make excuses (5,3,4)
9 Prying (5)
10 Burdensome (7)
11 Hard of hearing (4)
12 Woollies (8)
14 Things that happen (6)
15 Unpolished—ribald (6)
18 Condition such as housemaid's knee (8)
20 Oxidised iron (4)
22 Eighth planet from the sun (7)
23 Survive (5)
24 Film industry (collectively) (6,6)

Down

2 Atrophy—careless destruction (7)
3 Votes against (4)
4 Bristling with perplexities (6)
5 Ballot for public office (8)
6 Run away (to Gretna Green?) (5)
7 Cause (someone) to lose their bearings (12)
8 Unexpected advantage (2,5,5)
13 Settled way of thinking (8)

16 Typical—in utero (anag) (7)
17 Tendons (6)
19 Disgust (5)
21 Expensive—honey (4)

Solution no 37

Quick crossword no 39

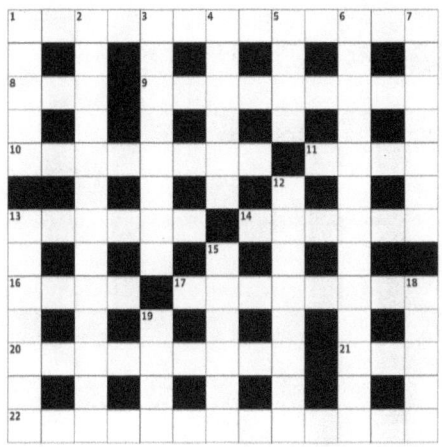

Across

1 Win a race (6,3,4)
8 Pull (3)
9 Concerning (2,7)
10 Don't mention it! (3,2,3)
11 Make well (4)
13 Used the horn (6)
14 Deny any connection with (6)
16 Time period (4)
17 Refusing to come to terms with a painful reality (2,6)
20 Useful facilities (9)
21 Enjoyment (3)
22 In good shape (4,3,6)

Down

1 Conductor's wand (5)
2 Scottish dance (9,4)
3 Skimpy knickers (8)
4 Excitement (6)
5 Ova (4)
6 Stop trying to persuade someone that you are right and they are wrong (5,2,6)
7 Greek letter (7)

12 Movie buff—tie canes (anag) (8)
13 Track beside a canal (7)
15 Relax (6)
18 Gangling (5)
19 Kind of bean (4)

Solution no 38

Quick crossword no 40

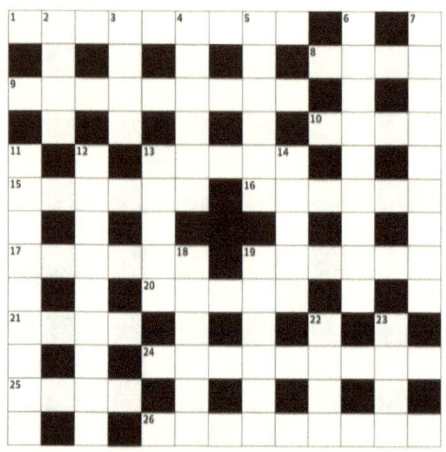

Across

1. Savagery (9)
8. Well I never! (4)
9. Shut up shop (5,4)
10. Flog (4)
13. Peculiar (5)
15. One of the Twelve Apostles (6)
16. Cowardly (6)
17. Northern girls? (6)
19. Pieces (6)
20. Light theatrical entertainment (5)
21. Incline (4)
24. Italian restaurant (9)
25. Rabbit (4)
26. Names of the most promising applicants for a job, selected for further consideration (9)

Down

2. Part in a play (4)
3. Audition (4)
4. Convenience (6)
5. Showy without taste or worth (6)
6. Let the cat out of the bag (4,5)
7. Cover-up—wall coating (9)

11. Sports—cheat list (anag) (9)
12. Seaboard (9)
13. Adam's ale (5)
14. Two in cards or dice (5)
18. Look for (6)
19. It's our (anag)—admirer (6)
22. Play tenpins (4)
23. X (4)

Solution no 39

Quick crossword no 41

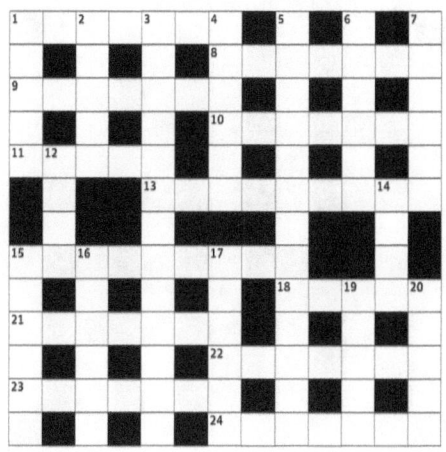

Across

1 Circular (7)
8 Inspiring fear (7)
9 Kite ban (anag)—bohemian (7)
10 Apostolic letter (7)
11 Long-handled spoon for serving soup (5)
13 No longer scheduled (9)
15 Revive (something) (9)
18 Turn aside (5)
21 Person keeping watch (7)
22 Sent out (7)
23 Waterfall (7)
24 Dog of mixed breed (7)

Down

1 Defamation (5)
2 Give, as an honour (5)
3 Junior NCO in the British Army (5,8)
4 Hire (4,2)
5 Strict organisation and control (13)
6 Building providing cheap overnight accommodation (6)
7 Stand up for (6)

12 Tool for shaping large pieces of wood (4)
14 Always (4)
15 Objects of historical interest (6)
16 Partner in marriage (6)
17 High regard (6)
19 Penetrate (5)
20 Ebbing and flowing (5)

Solution no 40

Quick crossword no 42

Across

1 Parched (2,3,2,4)
9 Agitated (2,7)
10 Spoil (3)
11 Led an (anag)—antelope (5)
13 Long-lasting—sea legs (anag) (7)
14 Trouble constantly (6)
15 Bring to an end (6)
18 Sirius (3,4)
20 Lobster or crab roe (5)
21 Descendant (3)
22 Absolve (9)
24 Formally submitted (4,3,4)

16 Under control (2,5)
17 Ornamental clasp (6)
19 Pay for—minister to—deal with (5)
23 Reverential fear (3)

Down

2 Pose for an artist (3)
3 Ornamental screen behind a church altar (7)
4 Hooded waterproof jacket (6)
5 Musical instruction to play gently and sweetly (5)
6 Wine steward (9)
7 Perish (4,3,4)
8 Skid lid (5,6)
12 Overbearing pride (9)

Solution no 41

Quick crossword no 43

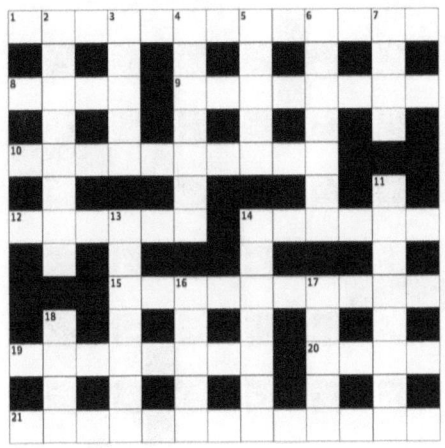

Across

1 Simultaneously (2,3,4,4)
8 An arm and a leg? (4)
9 Sardinian capital (8)
10 Fashionable (3,3,4)
12 Main course (6)
14 Hothead (6)
15 Share out (10)
19 Lack of any false pride (8)
20 Ornamental fabric (4)
21 Find ways of getting round regulations (4,3,6)

17 Invoices (5)
18 Regular hexahedron (4)

Down

2 Of little importance (8)
3 Addiction to a drug (5)
4 Small northern Pacific salmon (7)
5 Hot molten rock (5)
6 Hindmost part (4,3)
7 Extra (4)
11 Tiny amount (8)
13 Fit of extreme anger (3,4)
14 Persons suffering for their beliefs (7)
16 Worker in metals (5)

Solution no 42

Quick crossword no 44

Across

1 Silence! (4)
3 Tropical plant producing peppers—music cap (anag) (8)
8 Disdainful pout (4)
9 Ponder on (8)
11 Someone who looks very like another (4,6)
14 O, great! (anag)—a worthless fellow (6)
15 French fashion designer and perfumier, d. 1971 (6)
17 Having a resonant metallic sound (10)
20 Twig (6,2)
21 Rule Britannia's composer, d. 1778 (4)
22 Comic verse (8)
23 Pulses (4)

Down

1 Dampness (8)
2 Informer (what a swine!) (8)
4 Quantity (6)
5 Association of women linked by a common interest (10)
6 Yield (4)
7 Sort of brandy made from the remains of pressed grapes (4)
10 Burst forth (5,5)
12 Following the correct route (2,6)
13 Acts in a conceited way (8)
16 No longer fastened (6)
18 Sour to the taste (4)
19 For men only (4)

Solution no 43

Quick crossword no 45

Across

1 Duke of 21's horse at Waterloo—capital city (10)
7 Parts of speech—poor nuns (anag) (8)
8 Greek aniseed liqueur (4)
9 Arrangement for deferred payment (4)
10 Unpaid debts (7)
12 Capital city—uneasier sob (anag) (6,5)
14 Interminable (7)
16 Habitual drunk (4)
19 Bonce (4)
20 Extremely agitated—if recent (anag) (8)
21 Kind of boot (10)

Down

1 French landscape painter, d. 1875 (5)
2 Flamboyant style (7)
3 Common sense (4)
4 Hitler's nationality pre-1925 (8)
5 Bring to mind (5)
6 Portuguese North Atlantic islands (6)
11 Swollen-headed (8)
12 Decrepit old car (6)
13 Minaret (anag)—clothing (7)
15 Provide accommodation for (5)
17 Pungent vegetable (5)
18 Penny-pinching (4)

Solution no 44

Quick crossword no 46

Across

1 Refute (10)
7 Spiked attachment for a climbing boot (7)
8 Council of the clergy (5)
10 Putrid (4)
11 Negligent (8)
13 Fire-breathing monster (6)
15 Cover for holding loose papers together (6)
17 Aesthetically pleasing (8)
18 Tiresome person—tidal flood (4)
21 Obtuse—impenetrable (5)
22 Tool with hooks for grasping and holding (7)
23 Caught by surprise—I did blends (anag) (10)

Down

1 22 yards (5)
2 Back of the neck (4)
3 Learnt (anag)—lease (6)
4 Word blindness (8)
5 Maintain (7)
6 Certified officially (10)

9 Unruly (10)
12 Expected (8)
14 Weapons store (7)
16 Old Testament book (6)
19 Had—endow (anag) (5)
20 Unyielding (4)

Solution no 45

Quick crossword no 47

Across

1 Flag—of the usual kind (8)
5 Competent (4)
9 Peers of the realm (5)
10 Vanity (7)
11 Soldiers regarded as expendable in battle (6,6)
13 Perplexed—rotten (6)
14 Exactly right (4,2)
17 Unbearable (12)
20 Beyond endurance (3,4)
21 Strident sound (5)
22 Established standards (4)
23 Marvellous (8)

16 Chess piece (6)
18 Throng (5)
19 Tear apart (4)

Down

1 Lather (4)
2 Gauche—obstinate (7)
3 Not sincere (12)
4 Modern—centre (anag) (6)
6 Procreate (5)
7 Install as a 16 (8)
8 Ill-matched (12)
12 Imperial (8)
15 Manx parliament (7)

Solution no 46

Quick crossword no 48

Across

1 Writing table (4)
3 Honest (8)
9 Work out in more detail (7)
10 One with a very thick skin (abbr) (5)
11 Underground chapel (5)
12 First-born (6)
14 Fizz (13)
17 Greek messenger of the gods (6)
19 Last letter of the Greek alphabet (5)
22 Fruit of the oak (5)
23 Greek god of wine (7)
24 Merited (8)
25 Walk wearily (4)

16 Best—selection (6)
18 Country seat (5)
20 Lethe (anag)—Barrymore or Merman (5)
21 Group of musicians (4)

Down

1 Taken off (8)
2 Astute (5)
4 Deserving censure (13)
5 Worn out (5)
6 Shiver of excitement (7)
7 Coil (4)
8 Alerts (anag)—building worker (6)
13 Got worse again (8)
15 UK shipping forecast area (7)

Solution no 47

Quick crossword no 49

Across

1 Kitchen utensil (4,5)
8 Behave theatrically (5)
9 One with personal attractiveness (7)
10 Person kept in custody (8)
11 Brandenburg Concertos composer, d. 1750 (4)
13 Simpleton—pasta (6)
14 Bad-tempered complainant (6)
16 Place for keeping racing pigeons (4)
17 Group of rowdy young American film stars of he 1980s (4,4)
19 Leaves the house (4,3)
20 Gallery for works of art—loans (anag) (5)
21 Alternate (4,5)

Down

1 Pliant (8)
2 Small soft container—a chest (anag) (6)
3 Mop (4)
4 Limitless (12)
5 Of seismic proportions (5-7)
6 Influential member (7,5)

7 One with a compulsive desire to manipulate others (7,5)
12 Raises objection (8)
15 Kitchen utensil (6)
18 Outer garment (4)

Solution no 48

Quick crossword no 50

Across

- **1** Huggable (6)
- **4** Turned—malodorous (6)
- **8** Above the horizon (5)
- **9** Absurd pretence (7)
- **10** Supervise (7)
- **11** Impossible (3,2)
- **12** Awarded medals (9)
- **17** Criminal (5)
- **19** European Union's most southerly capital (7)
- **21** Educational institution (7)
- **22** Tartan cloth (5)
- **23** Herb tea (6)
- **24** Trapped (6)
- **14** Hopelessness (7)
- **15** Remnant (6)
- **16** Praised (6)
- **18** Sprawls (5)
- **20** Castrated chicken (5)

Down

- **1** Incentive (6)
- **2** Bloat (7)
- **3** Golf course by the sea (5)
- **5** Opposing (7)
- **6** Repeated rhythmic phrase (5)
- **7** (Spanish) chaperone (6)
- **9** Intervening space (9)
- **13** Institutional eating place (7)

Solution no 49

Quick crossword no 51

Across

5 Clothes for casual activities (11)
7 Outlay (4)
8 Artificially high singing voice (8)
9 Judge to be probable (5,2)
11 Ruffle (5)
13 Fawn (5)
14 Thief (slang) (3,4)
16 Abuse (8)
17 Game counter representing money (4)
18 Believing in equal opportunities (11)

Down

1 Highland dress (4)
2 Clown (7)
3 Answer (5)
4 Intellectual (8)
5 Appear as old as one is (4,4,3)
6 Vengeance (11)
10 Drink before bedtime (8)
12 Supporting male actor at a wedding (4,3)
15 Moderately warm (5)
17 Metal currency (4)

Solution no 50

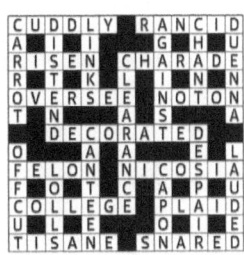

Quick crossword no 52

Across

5 Resist (9)
8 Soon (4)
9 Testimony—verification (8)
10 UK shipping forecast area (6)
11 Shady garden alcove (6)
13 Cause to be loved (6)
15 Cry—snitch (6)
16 Unwelcome visitor (8)
18 Food (for a friar?) (4)
19 Savagely fierce (9)

Down

1 Highest point (8)
2 Joyful—optimistic (6)
3 King of the Huns, d. 453 (6)
4 Leg joint (4)
6 Angered by unjust treatment (9)
7 Residence (9)
12 Utter impulsively (5,3)
14 Very exciting—glowing (3-3)
15 Morally degraded (6)
17 South American flightless bird (4)

Solution no 51

Quick crossword no 53

Across

1 One who fails to hold a catch (13)
8 Gods (7)
9 Make fun of (5)
10 Fuel (4)
11 Infatuated (8)
13 Prescribed ceremony (6)
14 Very weak (6)
17 New Year's Eve for Scots (8)
19 Gold-coloured (4)
21 Growl viciously (5)
22 Panther (7)
24 Conceited (7-6)

16 Large oceanic sport fish (6)
18 Seabird excrement, once prized as fertiliser (5)
20 Circular pyramid (4)
23 Broken (3)

Down

1 Offer a price (3)
2 Dense shrubbery (7)
3 Morally wrong (4)
4 Decay (6)
5 Main element of air (8)
6 Perform (5)
7 Best-balanced—it's sedate (anag) (9)
10 Liver disease (9)
12 Imaginary line round the Earth (8)
15 Robber—darn big (anag) (7)

Solution no 52

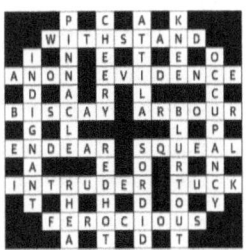

Quick crossword no 54

Across

1 Horrified (6)
4 Less in number (5)
7 Fruit (6)
8 Stimulus (6)
9 Young elephant (4)
10 Object of abhorrence (8)
12 Young hooligans (11)
17 One present at an event (8)
19 Spanish painter, d. 1828 (4)
20 Insubstantial (6)
21 County town of Devon (6)
22 Snag (5)
23 Social position—prestige (6)

15 Diffidence (7)
16 Affection (6)
18 Cardinal point (5)

Down

1 Give an ovation (7)
2 Co-operative (7)
3 Long drawn-out (9)
4 Deceptive manoeuvre (5)
5 Most crafty (7)
6 Annul an act of parliament (6)
11 Light-hearted pastime (9)
13 Uproot by force (7)
14 Treat carelessly (7)

Solution no 53

Quick crossword no 55

Across

1 Flung (6)
4 Rules or regulations adopted by an organisation (6)
9 Brief and to the point (7)
10 Short surplice worn by Catholic priests—to act (anag) (5)
11 Stratospheric layer of gas—invigorating sea air (5)
12 Lured (7)
13 Timeless cob (anag)—food (11)
18 My house in France? (4,3)
20 Partial or comparative darkness (5)
22 Lubricated (5)
23 Soon (poetically) (7)
24 Group of seven performers (6)
25 Provide with garments (6)

Down

1 Browbeat (6)
2 Beatles drummer (5)
3 Look with the power to inflict harm (4,3)
5 Sailing vessel (5)
6 The—thing (7)

7 Beer and lemonade mixture (6)
8 Building site revolver? (6,5)
14 Coincide partly (7)
15 Samuel Johnson's biographer (7)
16 Horizontally (6)
17 Popular music of Jamaican origin (6)
19 Tiny fly (5)
21 Approximately (5)

Solution no 54

Quick crossword no 56

Across

1. Controversial issue attracting public attention (5,7)
9. Granny Smith, for one (5)
10. Type of lettuce (7)
11. Lie to get something (4)
12. Building divided into small let units (8)
14. Playing a part (6)
15. Sheep from Spain with a heavy quality fleece (6)
18. Latest time for completion (8)
20. Flower—girl (4)
22. Florida resort—Virginia Woolf novel (7)
23. Heavy iron-bound stick used for crowd control by police in India (5)
24. Canadian province (3,9)

Down

2. Road-surfacing material (7)
3. Outhouse—cast (4)
4. Bird with a long curved bill (6)
5. Palm tree (anag)—south Wales university town (8)
6. Groom's partner (5)
7. Method for removing unwanted hair (12)
8. Devoted old married couple (5,3,4)
13. Quick joke (3-5)
16. Crackbrained (7)
17. In utero (6)
19. Acknowledge—concede (5)
21. Defect (4)

Solution no 55

Quick crossword no 57

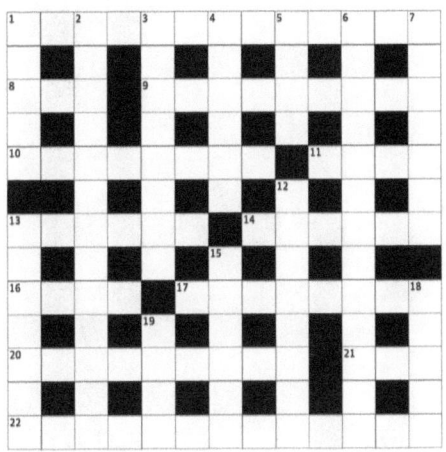

Across

1 Before you can say Jack Robinson (5,2,1,5)
8 Muhammad___(or MacGraw?) (3)
9 Pitch in (4,1,4)
10 Naughtiness (8)
11 The Buckeye State (4)
13 Organic fertiliser (6)
14 Runcible eating irons? (6)
16 Average—standard (4)
17 Angels (8)
20 Yowl (9)
21 Exclude (3)
22 Take very great risks (4,4,5)

15 Formally reject a former belief (6)
18 Undergo transformation (5)
19 Become bigger (4)

Down

1 Misgiving (5)
2 Quirky (13)
3 Desert of south-west Africa (8)
4 Abrasive tool (6)
5 Apartment (4)
6 Morbid fear of spiders (13)
7 Ugly (7)
12 Aghast (8)
13 Threatened (7)

Solution no 56

Quick crossword no 58

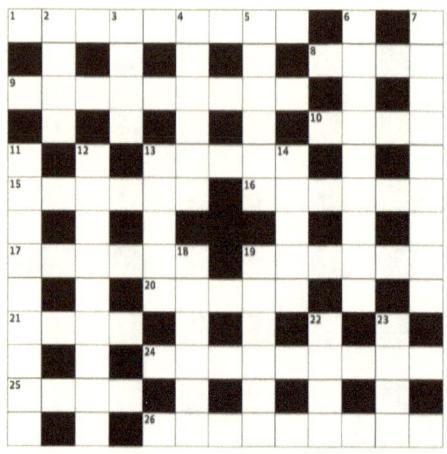

Across

1 Maritime disaster (9)
8 Seaside structure (4)
9 Entrance hall (9)
10 Instruction to stop (4)
13 Film (5)
15 Servile follower (6)
16 Soft drink (6)
17 Excessive (French) (2,4)
19 Highly seasoned sausage (6)
20 Heartless (5)
21 Given the chop (4)
24 Design or guide for making something (9)
25 Completely ended (4)
26 Skill in a particular field (9)

Down

2 Hastened (4)
3 Cooking utensils (4)
4 Walter Scott novel (3,3)
5 French channel port (6)
6 Immediately (5,4)
7 Inhale (7,2)
11 Colosseum combatant (9)

12 Strewn (9)
13 Red wine from an area of southwest France (5)
14 Peer (5)
18 Verbose (6)
19 Rigorous—harsh (6)
22 Horse's gait (4)
23 Burden—responsibility (4)

Solution no 57

Quick crossword no 59

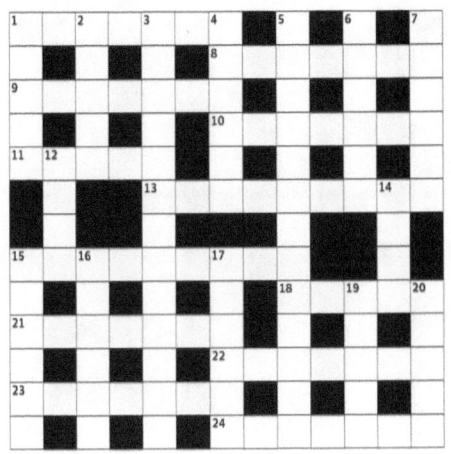

Across

1 Small dried seedless grape (7)
8 Meatier (anag)—Qatar, for example (7)
9 Deficiency of red blood cells (7)
10 Globes (7)
11 Stinking (5)
13 Without doubt (9)
15 Declared to be a saint (9)
18 Roughage (5)
21 Hormone produced in the pancreas (7)
22 Copy (7)
23 One of Harpo's brothers (7)
24 Mischievousness—rascally tricks (7)

Down

1 Banter—corn husks (5)
2 Cook in an oven (5)
3 War (5,8)
4 Tricky question (6)
5 Scottish dance (8,5)
6 French president (6)
7 Liverpool's river (6)
12 __ Pound, American poet (4)

14 Shakespearean king (4)
15 Cower (6)
16 One who fails to arrive (2-4)
17 Elder (6)
19 Courageous (5)
20 Adversary (5)

Solution no 58

Quick crossword no 60

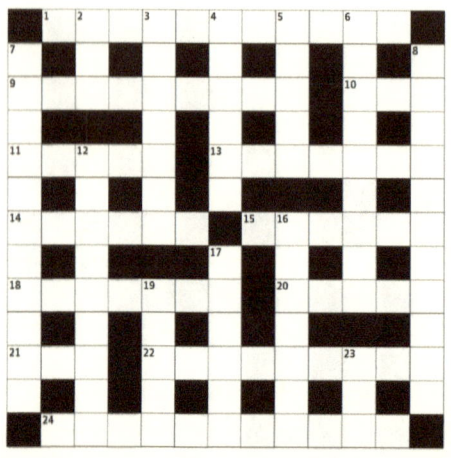

Across

1 Extended built-up area (11)
9 I have no idea! (4,3,2)
10 Storage container (3)
11 Easily understood (5)
13 Section (anag)—spots (7)
14 Broken pieces of pottery (6)
15 Disappear (6)
18 Blow up (7)
20 Inexpensive (5)
21 Label—children's game (3)
22 Prestigious group of US universities (3,6)
24 Waterproof boots (11)

17 Native of Nairobi, perhaps (6)
19 Projecting bay window—Oxford college (5)
23 Information (3)

Down

2 Acknowledge (3)
3 Without assistance (7)
4 Skimpy bathing costume (6)
5 Larceny (5)
6 Aim (9)
7 Young people (11)
8 Chirping insect (11)
12 Sparkling wine (9)
16 Very old (7)

Solution no 59

Quick crossword no 61

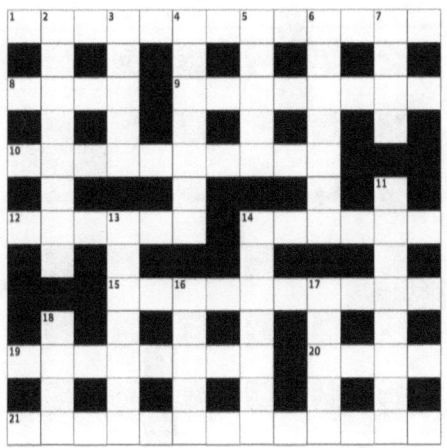

Across

1 Incorporating all the newest ideas and features (5,2,3,3)
8 Air pollution (4)
9 Convert from code into plain language (8)
10 District of Paris, associated with many artists (10)
12 Dessert (6)
14 Delicate and pale in colour (6)
15 (Product) for removing unwanted hair (10)
19 Culinary herb (8)
20 Water-filled defensive trench (4)
21 Rodent kept as a pet (6,7)

Down

2 Author of The Bonfire of the Vanities (3,5)
3 Inebriated (5)
4 Trying experiences (7)
5 Implied—inferred (5)
6 Articulate (7)
7 Tall woody grass (4)
11 Diminish (8)

13 Borne (7)
14 Cornmeal—on plate (anag) (7)
16 Heathen (5)
17 Weighty books (5)
18 Luminous sign of saintliness (4)

Solution no 60

Quick crossword no 62

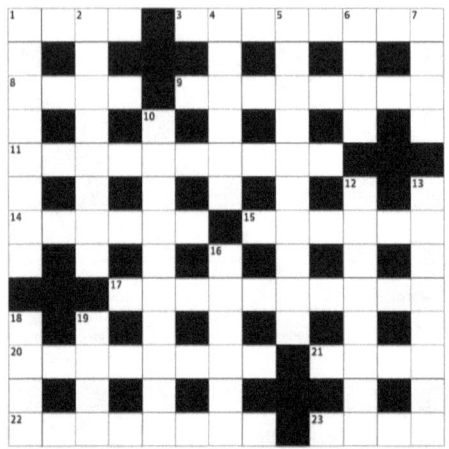

Across

1 Covering for the wrist (4)
3 Likened (8)
8 Relocate (4)
9 Non-military (8)
11 Fiendish (10)
14 Riches (6)
15 Middle (6)
17 Genealogical chart (6,4)
20 Improved (8)
21 Person regularly 'economical with the truth' (4)
22 Left over (8)
23 Regard lecherously (4)

13 Practise (8)
16 Filmdom (6)
18 Prickly adhesive seed case (4)
19 A long, long time (4)

Down

1 Loss of status (8)
2 Recommended consumption of fruit and veg (4,1,3)
4 Egyptian god, father of Horus (6)
5 Detective (7,3)
6 Incursion (4)
7 Unpleasantly wet and cold (4)
10 Smuggled goods (10)
12 Dying of hunger (8)

Solution no 61

Quick crossword no 63

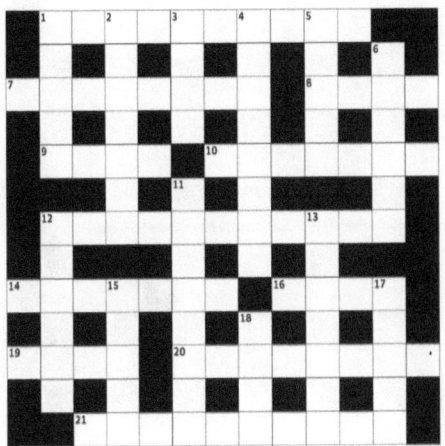

Across

1 Once popular child's toy— favourite topic (5,5)

7 Circumspection—girl's name (8)

8 Old-fashioned pronoun (4)

9 Spanker or spinnaker, for example (4)

10 Stupid (7)

12 Portuguese explorer d. 1524 (5,2,4)

14 Nimbleness (7)

16 Leave out (4)

19 Hit with the head (4)

20 The Prairie State (8)

21 Posh (5-5)

13 Pungent gas (7)

15 Illuminated (3,2)

17 Coin-tossing call (5)

18 Group of countries (4)

Down

1 Parsley, sage, rosemary and thyme (5)

2 Pals (7)

3 Tug (4)

4 Remain too long (8)

5 Prince of Darkness (5)

6 Part of the eye (6)

11 Slow-moving reptile (8)

12 Energy (6)

Solution no 62

Quick crossword no 64

Across

1 Annoying (10)
7 Exploded (5,2)
8 Asian country (5)
10 A lot (4)
11 Offer of marriage (8)
13 Noon (6)
15 (Draw with) a coloured stick (6)
17 Go into the red (8)
18 Swear (4)
21 Rope-making fibre (5)
22 Wild mountain sheep of Corsica—
   mono flu (anag) (7)
23 Two-story flat (10)

16 (Now mainly farmed) fish (6)
19 Worth (5)
20 Kick—bet—boat (4)

Down

1 Former PM (5)
2 Diminutive (4)
3 Run out (6)
4 Indoor footwear (8)
5 Self-deprecating quality (7)
6 Self-denying (10)
9 Omniscient (3-7)
12 Father of Icarus (8)
14 Taking place far from land (4-3)

Solution no 63

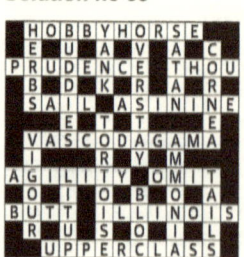

Quick crossword no 65

Across

1 Immense (8)
5 Restless desire (4)
9 Zirconium, for example (5)
10 Wise king of Israel (7)
11 Good enough (12)
13 Maintenance (6)
14 Desert-dwelling rodent (6)
17 Science of the properties of celestial bodies (12)
20 Hampered (7)
21 One who loafs about (5)
22 Tale (4)
23 Gloaming (8)

16 Follow secretly (6)
18 Drunkard (5)
19 (Of sparkling wine) extremely dry (4)

Down

1 Deciduous trees (4)
2 Proceeding as planned (2,5)
3 Small units of time (12)
4 Hazardous (6)
6 Musical speed (5)
7 One employed to do odd jobs (8)
8 Percussion instrument (12)
12 Boldness (8)
15 Arrears of work (7)

Solution no 64

Quick crossword no 66

Across

1 Sodium chloride (4)
3 Worked up (8)
9 Pariah (7)
10 Crosspieces fastened over the necks of a pair of draft animals (5)
11 Ridges of sand (5)
12 At once (anag) (6)
14 Tuber used in oriental cookery (5,8)
17 Make tea (4,2)
19 Doctrine to be accepted without question (5)
22 Loud resonant noise (5)
23 Faint notion (7)
24 Time without end (8)
25 Conspiracy (4)

Down

1 Decisive confrontation (8)
2 Classical language (5)
4 Stop waffling! (3,2,3,5)
5 Lovers' secret rendezvous (5)
6 Fooled—assimilated (5,2)
7 Prescribed amount (4)
8 German emperor (6)

13 Direct (8)
15 Connected row of houses (7)
16 Number puzzle (6)
18 Horse-drawn vehicle (5)
20 Interrogate (5)
21 Skin complaint (4)

Solution no 65

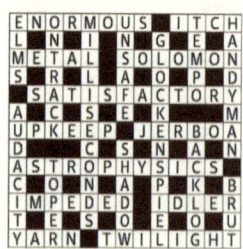

Quick crossword no 67

Across

1 Bottle opener (9)
8 Adult insect post-metamorphosis (5)
9 Warlike (7)
10 Incidentally (2,3,3)
11 Group of players (4)
13 Eraser (6)
14 Heavy non-venomous snake (6)
16 Auditory organs (4)
17 Counters (anag)—interpret (8)
19 Made possible (7)
20 Small wood (5)
21 Lasting a very short time (9)

15 Easy task (6)
18 In addition (4)

Down

1 Confined to a small space (8)
2 __ MacDonald, first British Labour PM (6)
3 Certain (4)
4 Make a lot of noise (5,3,4)
5 Polite (4-8)
6 Payment of money from a fund (12)
7 Coastal resort city in southern California (5,7)
12 Vision (8)

Solution no 66

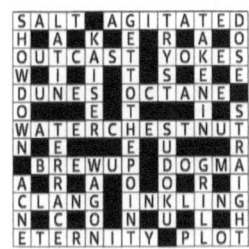

Quick crossword no 68

Across

1 Motionless (2,4)
4 Symbol (6)
8 Japanese cold rice dish (5)
9 Six-sided figure (7)
10 Cautious (7)
11 Male relative (5)
12 Rigidity (9)
17 Birds of prey (5)
19 Clergyman's house (7)
21 Green vegetable (7)
22 Scottish child (5)
23 Gracefully slender (6)
24 Feudal retainer (6)

15 Dissertation (6)
16 Book of church music (6)
18 Forgo (5)
20 Hooded snake (5)

Down

1 French wine region (6)
2 Holiday destinations (7)
3 Small light boat (5)
5 Assortment (7)
6 Reasoned thinking (5)
7 Fawlty Towers waiter (6)
9 Speak at length (4,5)
13 Jiffy (7)
14 Tales (7)

Solution no 67

Quick crossword no 69

Across

- **5** Excessively large amount (11)
- **7** One of the seven deadly sins (4)
- **8** In an off-hand manner (8)
- **9** Loose-fitting dress without a waist (7)
- **11** Ice cream portion (5)
- **13** Extra payment (5)
- **14** Minerva, for example (7)
- **16** Bat-and-ball game (8)
- **17** Make a reservation (4)
- **18** Unit of area (6,5)

Down

- **1** Remove the ovaries of a female animal (4)
- **2** Exact (7)
- **3** Partially melted snow (5)
- **4** Paid for (8)
- **5** Occurring at the same time (11)
- **6** First US national park, 1872 (11)
- **10** Lugubrious (8)
- **12** Disgusting—ie moons (anag) (7)
- **15** Acquire knowledge (5)
- **17** Wagers (4)

Solution no 68

Quick crossword no 70

Across

- **5** Eve of All Saints' Day (9)
- **8** Girl (of Richmond Hill?) (4)
- **9** Tea party—official function—heated argument (8)
- **10** Whine tearfully (6)
- **11** Annually (6)
- **13** Looked fixedly (6)
- **15** Small wave (6)
- **16** Homeric wanderer (8)
- **18** Sliding window frame (4)
- **19** Short work of fiction (9)

Down

- **1** Jewish festival celebrated in March or April (8)
- **2** Worldwide (6)
- **3** A score (6)
- **4** Fairy of Persian folklore (4)
- **6** Size (9)
- **7** Without offspring (9)
- **12** Relevant (8)
- **14** More profound (6)
- **15** Duty list (6)
- **17** (Fruit of the) blackthorn (4)

Solution no 69

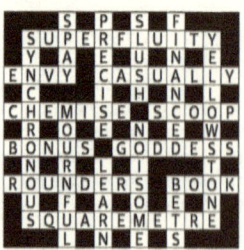

Quick crossword no 71

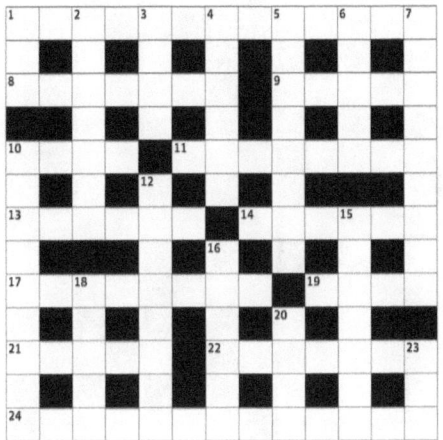

Across

1 Stealthy (13)
8 Lattice (anag) (7)
9 River of forgetfulness (5)
10 Inflamed swelling (4)
11 Precious metal (8)
13 Havoc (6)
14 Shut (6)
17 Strong drive for success (8)
19 Short extract from a film (4)
21 Poisonous (5)
22 Broadcasts—exposures (7)
24 Overdo (something) (5,2,6)

16 Independent principality on the French Riviera (6)
18 Pugilist (5)
20 Most important point (4)
23 Little sibling (3)

Down

1 Solidified (3)
2 Put right (7)
3 Surpassing the ordinary (4)
4 Threefold—singing voice (6)
5 Sneak (8)
6 Choose to participate (3,2)
7 Indignant (7,2)
10 Pompous—inflated (9)
12 US state, capital Frankfort (8)
15 Absence of sound (7)

Solution no 70

Quick crossword no 72

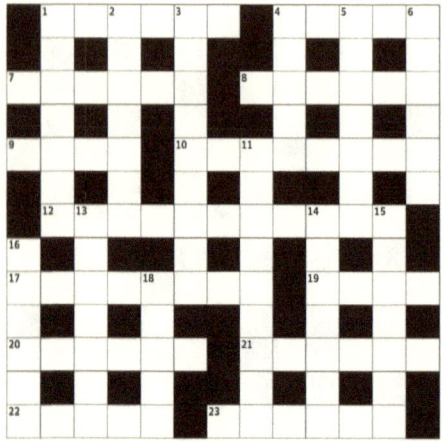

Across

1 Not so difficult (6)
4 Single figure (5)
7 Environment (6)
8 Rodent-catching cat (6)
9 Vivacity (4)
10 Made ready (8)
12 Work of outstanding artistry (11)
17 Obvious—clumsy (8)
19 Renown (4)
20 Gaffes (6)
21 Engrave (6)
22 Grass-like plant growing in wet places (5)
23 Stick one's oar in (6)

Down

1 Witty saying (7)
2 Mariners (7)
3 Kit (9)
4 Hang down loosely (5)
5 Pertaining to the stomach (7)
6 Diatribe (6)
11 Swear word (9)
13 Guaranteed (7)

14 Obliterated (7)
15 As a group (2,5)
16 New York borough (6)
18 Endured (5)

Solution no 71

Quick crossword no 73

Across

1 Remove weapons from (6)
4 Large—universal (6)
9 Sturdy 'British' dog (7)
10 Fed up (5)
11 Staunch (5)
12 Undergoing court process (2,5)
13 Dinner jacket worn with a white shirt (informal) (7,4)
18 Kenyan capital (7)
20 Irk (5)
22 Perch (5)
23 Anger at having been offended (7)
24 Work by Keats or Shelley, say (6)
25 Breathe out (6)

Down

1 Try something briefly and superficially (6)
2 Preposterous (5)
3 Sign of danger (or socialism)? (3,4)
5 Path around (5)
6 Gin and vermouth (7)
7 Hold close, affectionately (6)
8 Humiliating (11)

14 Embodiment (7)
15 Crate used by orators at Speakers' Corner? (7)
16 Deceive—lead on (6)
17 Painted or sculpted band running round under the ceiling (6)
19 External (5)
21 Tropical fruit with yellow skin and pink pulp (5)

Solution no 72

Quick crossword no 74

Across

1 Well-padded sofa with two arms and a back (12)
9 Arm off a larger body of water between headlands (5)
10 The Seagull's author (7)
11 Agreeable—subtle (4)
12 Correct procedure (8)
14 SI base unit of thermodynamic temperature (6)
15 Conundrum (6)
18 Micro-organisms associated with food poisoning (8)
20 Powder (abbr) (4)
22 Weather map lines (7)
23 Dislike intensely (5)
24 Kind of scheme aimed at making fast bucks (3-4-5)

7 Cavalier (5-3-4)
8 Like David against Goliath? (5-7)
13 Well-educated readers (8)
16 Vivid—explicit (7)
17 Tasteless art (6)
19 Tobacco—hooter (5)
21 Capital of Azerbaijan (4)

Down

2 Like the pattern on a snail's shell (7)
3 Fill totally (4)
4 Play it again! (6)
5 Brief (8)
6 Moral practice (5)

Solution no 73

Quick crossword no 75

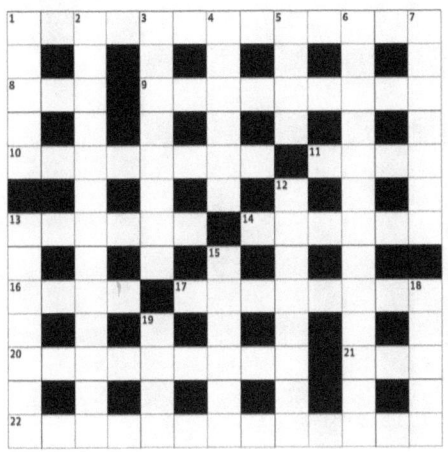

Across

1 A who's-the-daddy action (9,4)
8 Shoulder-to-wrist member (3)
9 Stewed meat in a thick white sauce (9)
10 Obsessed with a single subject (3-5)
11 Not a sausage (4)
13 Postpone (3,3)
14 Human (6)
16 Salmon-coloured (4)
17 Flat-sided fuel carrier (5,3)
20 Cantankerous (9)
21 Romanian money (3)
22 Building between The Mall and Trafalgar Square (9,4)

13 Powdered hot spice (7)

Down

1 Instrument with ivories (5)
2 Hissy fit (6,7)
3 Undesirable people (4-4)
4 Folly (6)
5 Chinese money (4)
6 Ordinary (13)
7 Loftier (anag)—clover-like plant (7)
12 Good manners (8)

Solution no 74

Quick crossword no 76

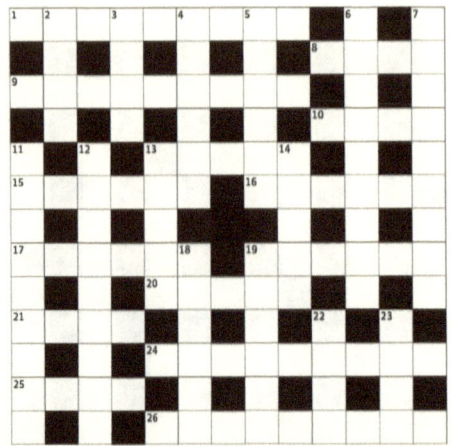

Across

1 Absolute belter (9)
8 Card—raiser (4)
9 Potential cause of harm from micro-organisms (9)
10 Killer whale (4)
13 Put to the sword (5)
15 Setting (6)
16 Evil imp (6)
17 Order restricting movements after a set time (6)
19 White whale (6)
20 Three-note chord—Chinese criminal gang (5)
21 Candle cord (4)
24 Powered equipment (9)
25 Father (4)
26 Deserted urban area (5,4)

Down

2 Separate part (4)
3 James and the Giant Peach author (4)
4 Rub noses (6)
5 Pincered insect (6)
6 Chatty (9)
7 From Kiev, say? (9)
11 Moving as hands do? (9)
12 Item filled in by a golfer (9)
13 Mixed rain and melting snow (5)
14 Moved slowly and cautiously forward (5)
18 The war (anag) (6)
19 Trite anticlimax (6)
22 Biting fly (4)
23 Extract (4)

Solution no 75

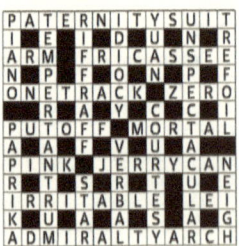

Quick crossword no 77

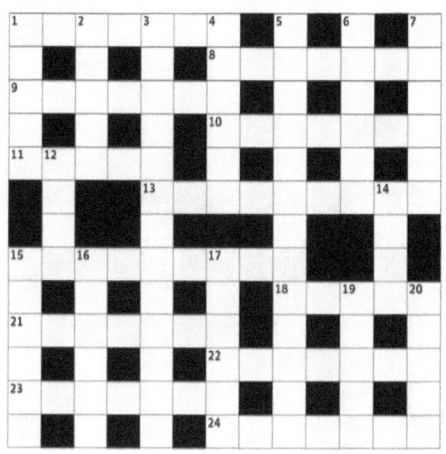

Across

1 Ignite again (7)
8 Route regularly used by commercial vessels (3,4)
9 Seed men (anag)—land attached to a property and retained for the owner's personal use (7)
10 Israeli city (3,4)
11 Feeling of dissatisfaction (5)
13 Where the king can't move (9)
15 Seville's region (9)
18 Anthropoid (5)
21 Paint-mixing board (7)
22 Moralist (7)
23 Material containing ferric metal (4,3)
24 How to cook chips (4-3)

Down

1 Long raised strip (5)
2 Fruit squeezed on Pancake Day? (5)
3 Hand signal? (13)
4 Type of fly (6)
5 Consume a huge amount of food (3,4,1,5)
6 Riga's country (6)
7 Artist's work (6)
12 Indian bread (4)
14 Roman garment (4)
15 Live-in young foreigner expected to do household chores (2,4)
16 Large shapeless lump (6)
17 Exuded (6)
19 Theme (5)
20 Fool (5)

Solution no 76

Quick crossword no 78

Across

1 Charades, for example (7,4)
9 Embedded (9)
10 Junk (3)
11 Soil's organic component (5)
13 Ledger for recording transactions as they occur (7)
14 Sudden arrival (of people or water?) (6)
15 Kiss and cuddle (6)
18 US state—Black Sea state (7)
20 Regal (5)
21 Sign of the zodiac (3)
22 Large broad-bladed weapon (9)
24 Men's underwear (5,6)

12 Venetian travel writer, who may (or may not) have served Kublai Khan, d. 1324 (5,4)
16 Dark cherry (7)
17 Carnivorous insect, which rests as if in prayer (6)
19 Part between sloping sides of a roof (5)
23 Relevant (3)

Down

2 Snake (3)
3 Negotiates between parties (7)
4 Disordered (6)
5 Devout (5)
6 Legends and sagas, in general (9)
7 The Lady with the Lamp, d. 1910 (11)
8 Person or organisation with an interest in something (11)

Solution no 77

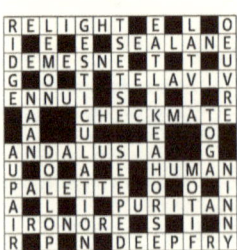

Quick crossword no 79

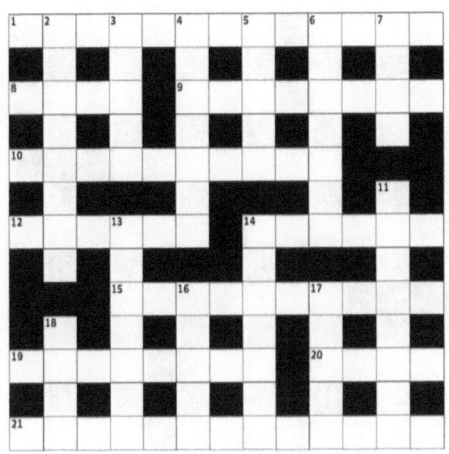

Across

1 Ridiculous combination of two figures of speech (5,8)
8 Gob (4)
9 Scornfully mocking (8)
10 Unquenchable (10)
12 Yes-man (6)
14 Champagne (informal) (6)
15 Financial security—teeters, say (anag) (4,6)
19 Large church building (8)
20 Early stringed instrument (4)
21 Clean-and-jerk sport (13)

16 Canonised person (5)
17 Fasten—engross (5)
18 Open jar for holding flowers (4)

Down

2 Exemption from punishment (8)
3 Additional (5)
4 Projectile (sometimes guided) (7)
5 Palpitate (5)
6 Adage (7)
7 Roman poet, d. about AD17 (4)
11 Lunar occurrence (which almost never happens) (4,4)
13 First—beginning (7)
14 Kind of long-grained rice (7)

Solution no 78

Quick crossword no 80

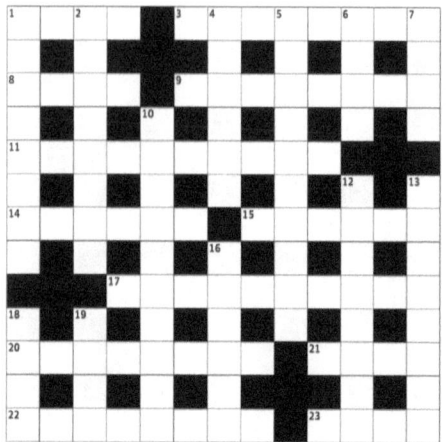

Across

1 Outdoor pool (4)
3 Total traffic jam (8)
8 Unit of electrical potential (4)
9 Cosmetic surgery to remove signs of aging (8)
11 Rich man with a much younger girlfriend (5,5)
14 Item of party food (6)
15 Vegetation-destroying grasshopper (6)
17 Striking (10)
20 Thick-ribbed trouser fabric (8)
21 Old sailors' tipple (4)
22 Orwellian language (8)
23 Cut a design into (4)

Down

1 Nauseatingly infatuated? (8)
2 Assiduous (8)
4 40th US president, d. 2004 (6)
5 Rastafarian hairstyle (10)
6 Short biography of someone who has died (abbr) (4)
7 Friends (4)

10 Three-step event (6,4)
12 Eruption (8)
13 Might (8)
16 Hindu or Buddhist temple (6)
18 Examine intensely—examine superficially (4)
19 Black bird (4)

Solution no 79

Quick crossword no 81

Across

1 The Hunchback of Notre-Dame author (6,4)

7 Actually present (2,6)

8 Julius Caesar's unlucky day in March (4)

9 Glandular secretion from a male deer, used in making perfume (4)

10 Go away (like a swarm?) (4,3)

12 Hot spot in the Mojave Desert, some of it 282ft below sea level (5,6)

14 Obstreperous (7)

16 Shivering fit (4)

19 Where coins were made (4)

20 Member of a former confederacy of six Native American peoples (8)

21 In the first place (10)

Down

1 Malice (5)

2 London football club (7)

3 Approximately (2,2)

4 Central American country, capital Tegucigalpa (8)

5 Garishness (5)

6 Interior of a steeple (where bats hang out?) (6)

11 Gigantic (8)

12 Particular (6)

13 Attempt, as a joke, to make somebody believe something that is not true (3-4)

15 Freshwater mammal with webbed and clawed feet (5)

17 Enlighten (5)

18 Soft feathers (like this clue) (4)

Solution no 80

Quick crossword no 82

Across

1 Self-governing American commonwealth in the Caribbean (6,4)

7 Person bringing charges (7)

8 Bout (5)

10 The Garden of England (4)

11 American thriller or detective movie style of the '40s and '50s (4,4)

13 Drink of the gods (6)

15 11am meal? (6)

17 Defamed (8)

18 You in olden times (4)

21 Cheeky (5)

22 President of Egypt, 1981-2011 (7)

23 In a position to reach a goal without much further difficulty (4,3,3)

Down

1 Nut tree of the southern United States and Mexico (5)

2 Direction taken when going from the US towards Ireland (4)

3 Pompous and boring (6)

4 Herb with narrow leaves (8)

5 Witty drawing (7)

6 Mule, for example (4,6)

9 Strong tremor (10)

12 Spout ending in a grotesquely carved figure (8)

14 Improvised song of the Caribbean (7)

16 Address of a religious nature (6)

19 Annoy continually (5)

20 Retired (4)

Solution no 81

Quick crossword no 83

Across

1 Diminutive folk hero (3,5)
5 Serious break in friendly relations (4)
9 From the Italian capital (5)
10 Mobster (7)
11 16th-century Spanish adventurer (12)
13 Warm up again (6)
14 Keen insight (6)
17 One way to leave a pirate ship for ever? (4,3,5)
20 Vibrating membrane in the head (7)
21 Regular (5)
22 Bluish shade of green (4)
23 Lineage (8)

Down

1 Sour—acid (4)
2 Enormous (7)
3 Animal's rear (12)
4 Fabric made with angora wool (6)
6 Did little or nothing (5)
7 Large tropical seedpod with tangy pulp—mad train (anag) (8)
8 Gardening (12)

12 Bully (8)
15 Search for a fugitive (7)
16 Dirty rats? (6)
18 Insect's feeding stage (5)
19 Have fun—theatrical work (4)

Solution no 82

Quick crossword no 84

Across

1 Turning point on which important developments depend (4)
3 Of the chest (8)
9 One who gives up too easily (7)
10 Briefs of two small panels connected by strings (5)
11 Complete (5)
12 In truth (6)
14 Lying between huge collections of stars—a critical gent (anag) (13)
17 Speak indistinctly (6)
19 Revise (3,2)
22 Little, charming and naughty (5)
23 Parthenogenetic (7)
24 Express grumpy opposition (8)
25 Small keyboarding error (4)

Down

1 Casserole of chicken pieces and onions in red wine (3,2,3)
2 Try to avoid (a problem) (5)
4 Oil-fuelled light with a glass chimney for outdoor use (9,4)
5 Highly valued (5)
6 Agreement (7)
7 Scuttler (4)
8 One gazing intently (6)
13 Mexican Pacific resort (8)
15 Until now (4,3)
16 Band worn for decoration (6)
18 Language group of southern Africa (5)
20 Flashy (5)
21 Netting (4)

Solution no 83

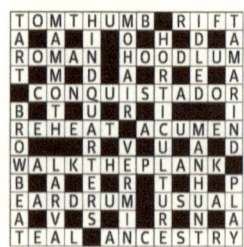

Quick crossword no 85

Across

1 The accused (9)
8 Poem of mourning (5)
9 Theatrical knife (7)
10 Brilliant (8)
11 Trim (4)
13 Light cavalry soldier (6)
14 Animal lacking pigment (6)
16 Notice (4)
17 On which scouts cook and around which they sing (8)
19 Obvious (7)
20 Pal (from Madrid?) (5)
21 1969 US rock festival (9)

12 Biscuit made with oats, syrup and butter (8)
15 Skin painting (6)
18 Red Planet (4)

Down

1 Deal with soiled clothing without water (3-5)
2 Joining together (6)
3 Tidy—without water (4)
4 Inflammation of a sac attached to the large intestine (12)
5 Booth used for making calls (9,3)
6 Raise a glass (4,3,5)
7 Female singing voice (5-7)

Solution no 84

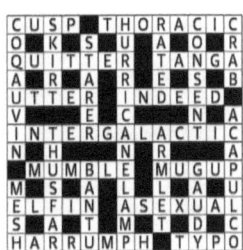

Quick crossword no 86

Across

1 Radiant—clever (6)
4 Vinegary (6)
8 Thin biscuit (5)
9 Make stronger (7)
10 In a moderately slow tempo (7)
11 Say baa! (5)
12 One who talks in an offensive way (9)
17 Muse of love poetry (5)
19 Edible root, eaten cooked—fils, say (anag) (7)
21 Hard-wearing twilled cloth—it's faun (anag) (7)
22 Glasses (abbr) (5)
23 Coming from Aden? (6)
24 Small animal with a pouch (6)

Down

1 Archer (6)
2 Unbeliever (7)
3 Wading bird (5)
5 North American reindeer (7)
6 Very short time (5)
7 North American wild dog (6)

9 Forenames (anag) (9)
13 Perfect (7)
14 Woman likely to succeed? (7)
15 Launch an attack on someone, verbally (3,3)
16 Mineral used to make plaster of Paris (6)
18 Tea-growing state in north-east India (5)
20 Cattle-catching rope (5)

Solution no 85

Quick crossword no 87

Across

- **5** The 18-yard box (7,4)
- **7** Green fruit—green colour (4)
- **8** Monument honouring the fallen (8)
- **9** Blue cheese (7)
- **11** Tired (5)
- **13** Fail (an exam, say) (5)
- **14** Succession of rulers from the same family (7)
- **16** Light cooking pot for camping (8)
- **17** Thai currency unit (4)
- **18** Inability to remember something that you normally can (6,5)

- **12** Eventually (2,3,2)
- **15** Get out of here! (5)
- **17** Lout (4)

Down

- **1** At a previous time (4)
- **2** Someone with the right to vote (7)
- **3** On the way out (5)
- **4** Abnormal redness of the skin—my heater (anag) (8)
- **5** Late 19th-century French style of painting using dots of colour (11)
- **6** Soviet Communist Party bureaucrat (11)
- **10** Home phone (8)

Solution no 86

Quick crossword no 88

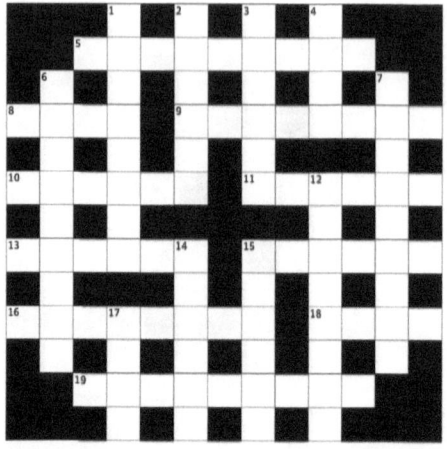

Across

5 Three-stringed instrument used to play Russian folk music (9)
8 Forearm bone (4)
9 Federal prison in California, 1934-63 (8)
10 Prone to chuckling (6)
11 One or the other (6)
13 Not a good person! (3,3)
15 Glitch (6)
16 Night light? (8)
18 Master (4)
19 Seemingly without limit (9)

17 Gas used in fluorescent lighting (4)

Down

1 Tirade (8)
2 Bright yellow shade (6)
3 Lacking social polish (6)
4 Parody (4)
6 Croc's close relative (9)
7 Preserve (9)
12 (Of a problem) difficult to handle and requiring great tact (8)
14 The Quiet American author (6)
15 Lecture on a moral topic (6)

Solution no 87

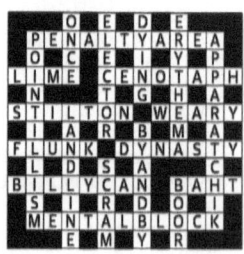

Quick crossword no 89

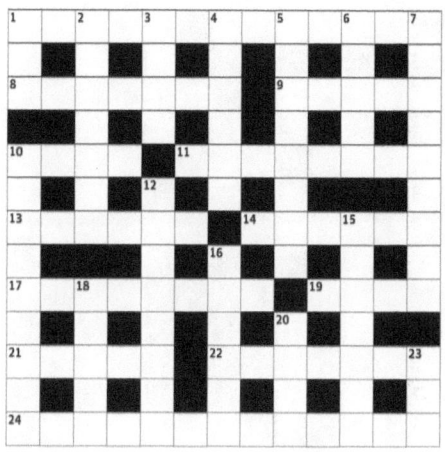

Across

1 Popular starter (5,8)
8 Low wall along a roof edge (7)
9 Lowest point (5)
10 Noise of a small object dropping into water (4)
11 Old campaigner (8)
13 Nervously restrained laugh (6)
14 Hitchcock's 1960 classic (6)
17 Event (8)
19 Expression of grief (4)
21 Large flow of liquid (5)
22 Those leaving their own country for political reasons (7)
24 Pell-mell (6-7)

7 Relating to theft (9)
10 Abraham or Isaac, perhaps (9)
12 French cop (8)
15 Guilty party (7)
16 Except if (6)
18 Not rude (5)
20 Gripper—fault (4)
23 Title for a baronet (3)

Down

1 Get-up-and-go (3)
2 Par trio (anag)—Charles de Gaulle, say (7)
3 Small bites (4)
4 Robin Hood figure? (6)
5 Capital of the Democratic Republic of the Congo (8)
6 Birch relative (5)

Solution no 88

Quick crossword no 90

Across

- **1** Well-dressed (6)
- **4** Sweet—hedge—evade (5)
- **7** Non-metallic element, C (6)
- **8** Little box (of strawberries?) (6)
- **9** Thin flat circular object (4)
- **10** Excessively (2,1,5)
- **12** Overwhelmingly impressive (4-7)
- **17** Convalescence (8)
- **19** Bigness (4)
- **20** Idea (6)
- **21** Increase the value (6)
- **22** High-ranking Turkish officer (5)
- **23** Food that's hard to digest (6)

Down

- **1** Arena (7)
- **2** Point of no return (which Caesar crossed in 49BC) (7)
- **3** PC (9)
- **4** Botch (5)
- **5** Legendary Spanish philanderer (3,4)
- **6** All of one's assets—5-door car (6)
- **11** Adviser on personal problems (5,4)
- **13** Stirs up (7)

- **14** Covered (7)
- **15** Official newspaper (7)
- **16** Financial agreement in case of divorce made by a couple before marriage (abbr) (3-3)
- **18** Stringed instrument tuned lower than a violin (5)

Solution no 89

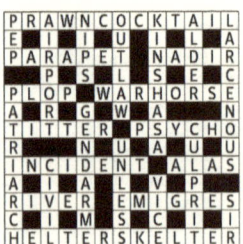

Quick crossword no 91

Across

1 Knock off (6)
4 Detestable (6)
9 Small cube of fried bread (7)
10 Ate (5)
11 Make painstaking enquiries (into something) (5)
12 Kill (7)
13 By its very nature (11)
18 Pig hurt (anag)—noble (7)
20 Lacerate (5)
22 Alec's (anag)—graduation (5)
23 Malicious hostility (7)
24 Mankind (6)
5 Scurry—small car (6)

Down

1 Reach a conclusion (6)
2 Whimsically comical (5)
3 Road safety device (7)
5 Needless (5)
6 Voluptuous (7)
7 Progress unsteadily (due to age?) (6)
8 Ceremony of conferring honours of rank on a person (11)

14 Bitter derision (7)
15 Failure to be there (7)
16 Sudden illegal acquisition of power (6)
17 Accumulation of electricity (6)
19 Envious—environmentalist (5)
21 Take as one's own (5)

Solution no 90

Quick crossword no 92

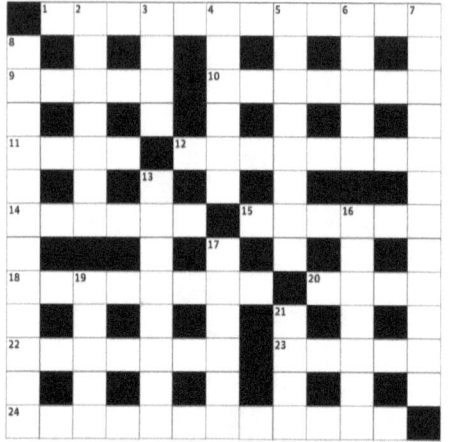

Across

1 In the intervals separating other activities (7,5)
9 Scope (5)
10 Confusion (7)
11 Small island in a river (4)
12 Impoverished—ending it (anag) (8)
14 Protective headgear (6)
15 Grapes (anag)—cigarette (slang) (6)
18 Much employed (4,4)
20 Immeasurably long period of time (4)
22 Blighty (7)
23 Customers (5)
24 Schoolchildren who return to an empty home (8,4)

13 Hand down (8)
16 Make believe (7)
17 Coastal department of western France (6)
19 Illumination (5)
21 Perform in the street for money (4)

Down

2 Involve (someone) in a dispute (7)
3 Unit of power—Scottish engineer, d. 1819 (4)
4 Stretch out (6)
5 Deadly (8)
6 North American elk (5)
7 Isolation (of a hermit?) (12)
8 Assume control of a situation (4,3,5)

Solution no 91

Quick crossword no 93

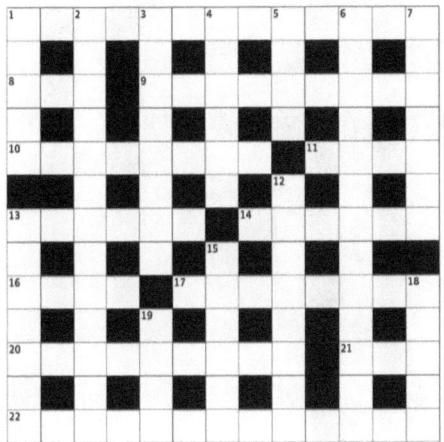

Across

1 The Rastafarian Messiah (5,8)
8 Crazy (3)
9 Scotch pancake (4,5)
10 Exhume (8)
11 Sister and wife of Zeus (4)
13 Golfer who can't drive straight? (6)
14 Author of Little Women, d. 1888 (6)
16 Hard work (4)
17 Large German dirigible (8)
20 Leader (9)
21 Metal, Sn (3)
22 Person with whom one shares common attitudes (7,6)

having a permanent one (3-4)
15 Running late (6)
18 Composition for nine instruments (5)
19 Morose (4)

Down

1 Moist (5)
2 Illness (13)
3 Put at risk (8)
4 Recalled (6)
5 Peas (anag)—part of a church (4)
6 Eventually (6,2,5)
7 Handsome (7)
12 Flimsy sandal (4-4)
13 Use any office workstation, not

Solution no 92

Quick crossword no 94

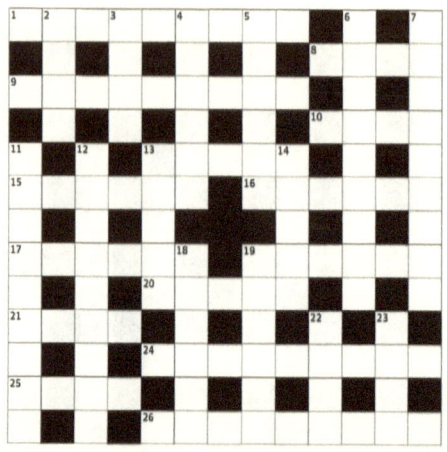

Across

1 Condemnation (9)
8 Be brave enough (4)
9 Unexpected but vivid recall of a past experience (9)
10 Finished (4)
13 Alarm—temptress (5)
15 Soldier serving on land and sea (6)
16 Unearth (3,3)
17 Holiday centre (6)
19 Pinched (6)
20 Showing signs of wear and tear (5)
21 Kernel (4)
24 Fortifying alcoholic drink (slang) (9)
25 Badger's burrow (4)
26 Method of execution (9)

Down

2 Govern (4)
3 Nonsense (4)
4 Taxi driver (6)
5 Holy (6)
6 Latin American dance (4,5)
7 Contrite (9)
11 Inexact (9)
12 Lying face downwards (9)
13 Inhale a recreational drug (5)
14 Particularly good (informal) (5)
18 Gossip (6)
19 Repress—itself (anag) (6)
22 Put right (4)
23 Stitched up (4)

Solution no 93

Quick crossword no 95

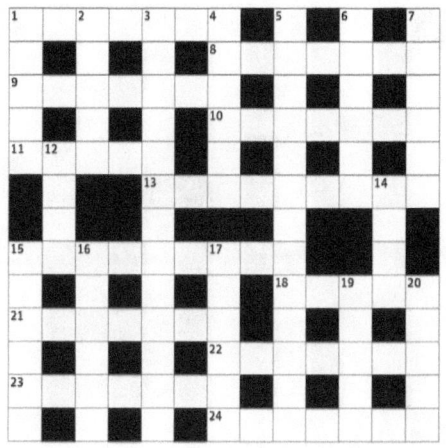

Across

1 Fabled one-eyed giant (7)
8 Body of troops arranged in a line (7)
9 Most humble (7)
10 Means of execution (3,4)
11 First premier of the Soviet Union, d. 1924 (5)
13 Based on personal accounts, possibly unreliable (9)
15 Stinks (9)
18 Praise (5)
21 Person from Barcelona? (7)
22 Young children's horses? (3-4)
23 Unintentional self-inflicted harm (3,4)
24 Give someone the right (7)

14 Florence's river (4)
15 Slightly crazy—bird (6)
16 Still in existence (6)
17 Confused interwoven mass (6)
19 (Make a) chirping noise (5)
20 (Fabric woven with) a fine cotton thread (5)

Down

1 Beast of burden (5)
2 Innocent (5)
3 Quite exceptional person (3,2,1,7)
4 Light upon (6)
5 Equestrian competition (5-3,5)
6 Very nearly (6)
7 Introduce publicly for the first time (6)
12 Per head (4)

Solution no 94

Quick crossword no 96

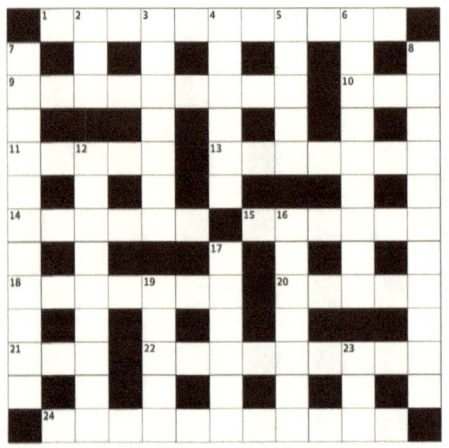

Across

1 Film or book making huge profits (11)
9 Staying power (9)
10 Yellowish-brown (3)
11 See how the land lies (informal) (5)
13 Put in order—organise (7)
14 The man (anag)—uplifting song (6)
15 Intellectual capacity (6)
18 Can be upheld (7)
20 Groom (oneself) with evident vanity (5)
21 Mongrel (3)
22 Volume of liquid used in cooking (9)
24 Has an unhappy outcome (4,2,5)

16 Ecstasy (7)
17 Take into custody (6)
19 Public swimming pool (5)
23 Distant (3)

Down

2 Boy (3)
3 Funeral procession (7)
4 Author of Pilgrim's Progress, d.1688 (6)
5 Remove fleece (5)
6 Far-reaching (9)
7 Coronary (5,6)
8 All the time (11)
12 Make a rapid escape (3,3,3)

Solution no 95

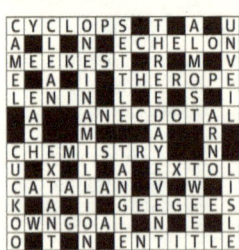

Quick crossword no 97

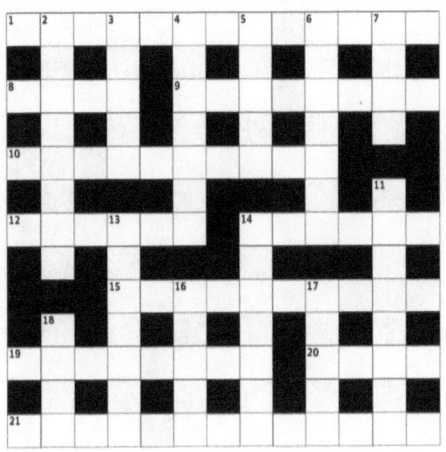

Across

1 Finished for ever (4,3,6)
8 Leguminous plant (4)
9 Head of a government department (8)
10 Number of those present (10)
12 Canadian province (6)
14 Provides what is required (6)
15 Rambling (10)
19 Painstakingly accurate (8)
20 Castle (4)
21 Skin specialist (13)

17 Body language of indifference (5)
18 Eat (4)

Down

2 Packed with incident (8)
3 Trip the light fantastic (5)
4 Itinerant (7)
5 West African country, formerly Dahomey (5)
6 Deference (7)
7 Paradise (4)
11 Foregoing (8)
13 Breach of social conventions (3,4)
14 Adviser (7)
16 Recce (5)

Solution no 96

Quick crossword no 98

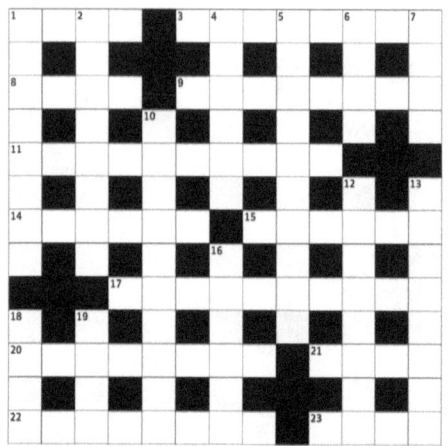

Across

1 End piece written for a piece of music (4)
3 Strikebreaker (8)
8 Note written as a reminder (4)
9 Roller-shaped object (8)
11 Dreamy—our UN goals (anag) (10)
14 Rough-and-tumble (6)
15 Alteration (6)
17 Fine and translucent (10)
20 Ordinary shares (8)
21 Just—blond (4)
22 Working dough (8)
23 Vendetta (4)

16 Bitterness—organ of the body (6)
18 Welsh national emblem (4)
19 Restore to good health (4)

Down

1 Finished (8)
2 Portray as evil (8)
4 Strata (6)
5 Lapdogs from Mexico (10)
6 Eye covers (4)
7 Clothing (4)
10 Not smart (4-6)
12 Use new ideas (8)
13 Used a blue pencil (8)

Solution no 97

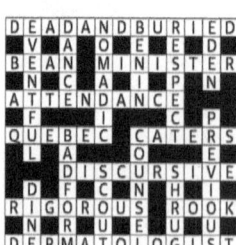

Quick crossword no 99

Across

1 Shortcoming (10)
7 The First State (to ratify the US constitution) (8)
8 Sly look (4)
9 Unpleasantly moist (4)
10 Losing one's hair (7)
12 In unison (3,8)
14 Curtains (7)
16 Stretch over (4)
19 Clubs (4)
20 Disease—a side bet (anag) (8)
21 With great courage (10)

17 Poor (5)
18 Plinth (4)

Down

1 Great fear (5)
2 Facecloth (7)
3 Applaud (4)
4 Lofty (8)
5 Managed well enough (5)
6 More eager (6)
11 Passage (8)
12 Out of the country (6)
13 Unlucky—he slaps (anag) (7)
15 Outdated (5)

Solution no 98

Quick crossword no 100

Across

1. Written works of merit (10)
7. Case for holding a light (7)
8. Publication (5)
10. Eat (slang)—food (slang) (4)
11. Struggle clumsily (8)
13. Deep sleep-like state (6)
15. Knight of the Round Table—the rag (anag) (6)
17. Loaded with regret (8)
18. Uncritically admired object (4)
21. Quaintly amusing (5)
22. Contagious skin infection (7)
23. Parched (10)

16. More intimate (6)
19. Wept (5)
20. Stop (4)

Down

1. School punishment (5)
2. Rain cats and dogs (4)
3. Cause continuing irritation (6)
4. Court of arbitration (8)
5. What's left (7)
6. Mean-spirited (3-7)
9. Quality of being gross (10)
12. In fact (8)
14. One name (anag)—plant (7)

Solution no 99

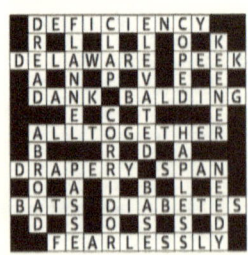

Quick crossword no 101

Across

1 Socially pretentious woman (4,4)
5 Party—clobber (4)
9 Thrash about (5)
10 Lustful (7)
11 Unfair (5,3,4)
13 Major blood vessel (6)
14 Doctor-priest working with magic (6)
17 Surfaced area for parking vehicles (12)
20 Most tidy (7)
21 Brideshead Revisited author, d. 1966 (5)
22 Adam and Eve's third son (4)
23 One who's owed money (8)

15 Organised search for a fugitive (7)
16 Synagogue official who conducts the liturgical part of the service (6)
18 Reprimand—cook (5)
19 Make a humming noise (4)

Down

1 Vitality (4)
2 Vernacular (7)
3 Starved (12)
4 Morally pure (6)
6 Love deeply (5)
7 Indecisive (8)
8 Presaged (12)
12 Great quantity (8)

Solution no 100

Quick crossword no 102

Across

1 Largest Caribbean island (4)
3 Sparkling wine (slang) (8)
9 Crossbred hunting dog (7)
10 Moderate glow (5)
11 Comply with (3,2)
12 Sway, as if about to fall (6)
14 Very close by (2,3,8)
17 Medium of divine revelation (6)
19 Slow speech with prolonged vowels (5)
22 Obliterate (5)
23 Meeting of a court (7)
24 Sauce for salad (8)
25 Outdoor festivity (4)

Down

1 Vocal ads (anag)—apple brandy (8)
2 Soft cap (5)
4 British admiral d. 21 October 1805 (7,6)
5 Strength (5)
6 Constituent—habitat (7)
7 Japanese wrestling (4)
8 As a consequence (6)

13 Conspicuous wealth (8)
15 Mayonnaise-based sauce with capers, eaten with fish (7)
16 Red cold salad ingredient (6)
18 Green cold salad ingredient (5)
20 Spry (5)
21 Be in want of (4)

Solution no 101

Quick crossword no 103

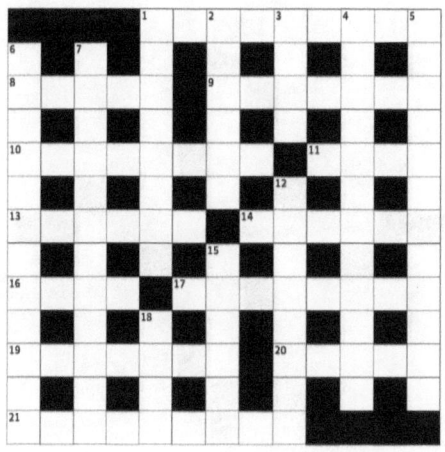

Across

1 Advocate (9)
8 Disordered state (5)
9 Destroy completely (4,3)
10 Originator (8)
11 Young salmon—a wife of Henry VIII (4)
13 Repaired (6)
14 Concealed (6)
16 Charitable donations to the needy (4)
17 Tepid (8)
19 Rouses from sleep (7)
20 Hymn of praise (5)
21 Abandonment (9)

Down

1 Calmly submissive (8)
2 Vocation (6)
3 Natural satellite of a planet (4)
4 Painter of A Bar at the Folies-Bergère, d.1883 (7,5)
5 Toppling of a king (12)
6 Oscar (7,5)
7 Resources for achieving something (4,3,5)

12 Gaping (4,4)
15 Breakfast cereal with fruits (6)
18 Make very hot and dry (4)

Solution no 102

Quick crossword no 104

Across

1 Artificial and inferior (6)
4 Sunglasses (informal) (6)
8 Subject set for discussion (5)
9 Prolonged artillery fire (7)
10 Widow Twankey's principal boy (7)
11 Execute mob-handed without trial (5)
12 Competitor about whose abilities little is known (4,5)
17 Spanish appetisers (5)
19 Act of imputing blame or guilt (7)
21 Most northerly town in the British Isles (7)
22 Inhumanly cruel person (5)
23 Savour—sauce (6)
24 Ice over (6)

Down

1 Bit players (6)
2 Attendant—wed star (anag) (7)
3 Have a prevailing direction (5)
5 Horse that races 'over the sticks' (7)
6 Bleed (5)
7 Smoulder (6)
9 Criterion (9)

13 Yokels (7)
14 Trap (7)
15 Alters (anag)—less fresh (6)
16 Carefree and happy (6)
18 Exposure to harm (5)
20 Highland Games event (5)

Solution no 103

Quick crossword no 105

Across

5 Gave in (11)
7 Tie (or what one puts in it?) (4)
8 Pass across (8)
9 Enduring energy (7)
11 Playing card (5)
13 Leather strap once used on Scottish schoolchildren (5)
14 Steer (7)
16 Tending (8)
17 Post (4)
18 Low-cut neckline (11)

Down

1 Notice—fictional puppy (4)
2 Drugs taken to reduce blood cholesterol (7)
3 Offering little hope (5)
4 Heavenly (8)
5 Reticent (11)
6 Very damaging (11)
10 Lose—limp case (anag) (8)
12 Turned sour (7)
15 Human joint (5)
17 Flesh as food (4)

Solution no 104

Quick crossword no 106

Across

5 Military training exercise (9)
8 Fastener (4)
9 Diving apparatus (8)
10 Go back to a former practice (6)
11 Followed (6)
13 State of health (6)
15 Perplex (6)
16 Pimp (8)
18 Is in session (4)
19 Portrayal (9)

Down

1 Most spiteful (8)
2 Lauren Bacall's first actor husband, d. 1957 (6)
3 Majestic—month (6)
4 Viva (4)
6 Become disillusioned (4,5)
7 As a matter of fact (2,7)
12 Brew (8)
14 Eavesdrop (informal) (6)
15 Scold (6)
17 Masticate (4)

Solution no 105

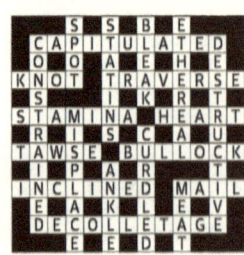

Quick crossword no 107

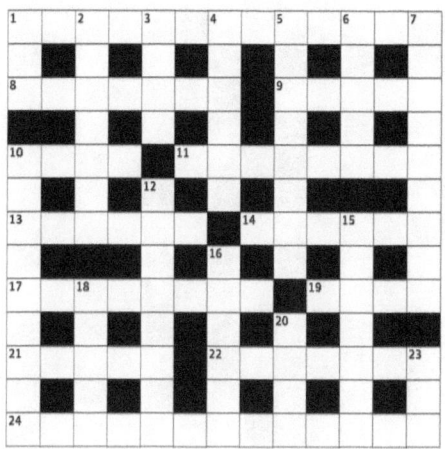

Across

1 Take by surprise (5,8)
8 Rack by a sink for letting crockery dry (7)
9 Scruffs of the neck (5)
10 Bundle (of hay?) (4)
11 Lazy (4-4)
13 Cloth in which a body is wrapped for burial (6)
14 Decapitate (6)
17 Indirect reference (8)
19 Level (4)
21 Cut into cubes (5)
22 Form a mental picture (7)
24 Without compunction, pity, or compassion (13)

Down

1 Rotter (3)
2 Short film advertising a forthcoming feature (7)
3 Suspend (4)
4 Constricted (6)
5 Itinerant (8)
6 Waterway where the current runs very fast (5)
7 Strap to hold up a stocking (9)
10 Onlooker (9)
12 Someone not accepted by society (8)
15 Draws out (7)
16 Relating to cattle (6)
18 Temporary replacement doctor (5)
20 Sugar merchant and art gallery philanthropist, founder, d. 1899 (4)
23 Cathedral city in East Anglia (3)

Solution no 106

Quick crossword no 108

Across

1 Death (6)
4 Funeral song (5)
7 Long tapering flag (6)
8 Wonderful or astonishing person (6)
9 Too (4)
10 Grannie's (anag)—income (8)
12 Instrument for determining the distance of an object (11)
17 Generosity (8)
19 Spindle (4)
20 Showy ornamental shrub (6)
21 Descend a cliff by rope (6)
22 Something valuable to have (5)
23 Historical records (6)

14 Lowest lake in the world (4,3)
15 Extended exchanges of tennis strokes (7)
16 Llama-like domesticated animal, valued for its wool (6)
18 Upstanding (5)

Down

1 Resident (7)
2 Rainy season in southern Asia (7)
3 Foolish (9)
4 Haggard (5)
5 Government's income (7)
6 Take the Queen's shilling (6)
11 Create a commotion (5,4)
13 Safety features in a motor car (3,4)

Solution no 107

Quick crossword no 109

Across

1 Wretchedness (6)
4 Wooden-headed hammer (6)
9 Become shrunken and wrinkled (7)
10 Unaccompanied (5)
11 Scare (anag) (5)
12 Passage selected from a larger work (7)
13 Three-card trick (4,3,4)
18 Beethoven piano concerto, Op. 73 (7)
20 Breast (5)
22 Speedy (5)
23 Amelia ___ , aviator, d. 1937 (7)
24 Most unrefined (6)
25 State capital of New South Wales (6)

Down

1 Unlucky accident (6)
2 More certain (5)
3 Prepared for exams (7)
5 Change to suit a new purpose (5)
6 Skin-tight garment (7)
7 Pact (6)

8 Lincolnshire seaside resort—lecher's poet (anag) (11)
14 Stated indirectly (7)
15 Freedom (7)
16 Gas-fired water heater (6)
17 Forge (6)
19 Evaluates the importance (of something) (5)
21 Killed (5)

Solution no 108

Quick crossword no 110

Across

1 Heart specialist (12)
9 Lifeless (5)
10 Cases (7)
11 Yanks (4)
12 Intermittently (2,3,3)
14 Extreme fear (6)
15 To an equal extent (2,4)
18 Cures (8)
20 Star Wars warrior (4)
22 Minty sweets (7)
23 Roosting place (5)
24 Commendable (12)

17 Playground item (6)
19 Venomous African snake (5)
21 Stimulus (4)

Down

2 One who retaliates—engrave (anag) (7)
3 Show excessive affection (4)
4 Accessible via the internet (6)
5 Cathedral musician (8)
6 Its state capital is Boise (5)
7 Shakespeare play (7,5)
8 Totalitarian regime (12)
13 State of inactivity or stagnation (8)
16 Dig up (7)

Solution no 109

Quick crossword no 111

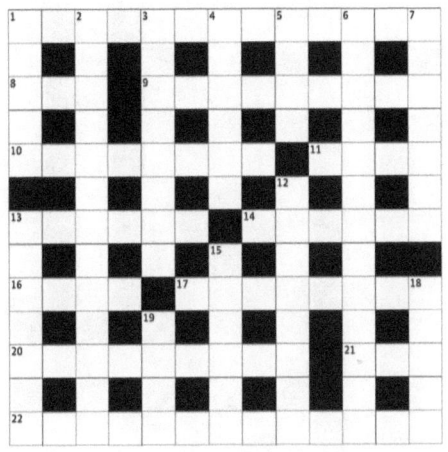

Across

1 Reprimand (4,3,1,5)
8 Assam or Darjeeling, for example (3)
9 Female singing voice (9)
10 People expected to fail (2-6)
11 Seed of a leguminous plant (4)
13 Pub (slang) (6)
14 Tail bone (6)
16 Shed excess weight (4)
17 Item of luggage (8)
20 Complain in the strongest possible terms (5,4)
21 Unit of measurement of thermal insulation in duvets, coats etc (3)
22 Extremely disappointed (4,2,1,6)

Down

1 Colossus (5)
2 (Of a drug) lowering sexual urges—Rio's a handicap (anag) (13)
3 Lived in (8)
4 Glad rags (6)
5 Visit various websites (4)
6 Fairground ride (6,7)
7 Legendary bird—Arizona city (7)

12 Mexican pancake (8)
13 Informal restaurants (7)
15 Discoverer's triumphant cry (6)
18 Oxygen's atomic number (5)
19 Greek cheese (4)

Solution no 110

Quick crossword no 112

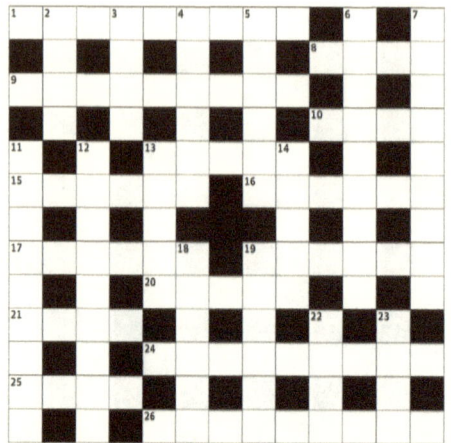

Across

1 Laugh uncontrollably (4,5)
8 Discontinue—delivery (4)
9 Provided solace (9)
10 Distinctively sharp taste (4)
13 Assistants (5)
15 Conclusion (6)
16 Elephant in a song (6)
17 Old and dusty spider's trap (6)
19 Walking (2,4)
20 Elevate (5)
21 Simple board game, involving dice (4)
24 Contented (9)
25 The Mormon state (4)
26 Brass instruments (9)

Down

2 River flowing through Shakespeare's Stratford (4)
3 Elevator (4)
4 Golf score of one stroke under par (6)
5 Inconsistent in quality (6)
6 Type of carpet—a bold Moor (anag) (9)

7 Type of pasta (9)
11 Rather poorly (3,6)
12 Very poorly (2,1,3,3)
13 Change (5)
14 French river (5)
18 Charity sale of many different things (6)
19 Densest of all naturally occurring metallic elements, Os (6)
22 In that case ... (2,2)
23 Lake—French mother (4)

Solution no 111

Quick crossword no 113

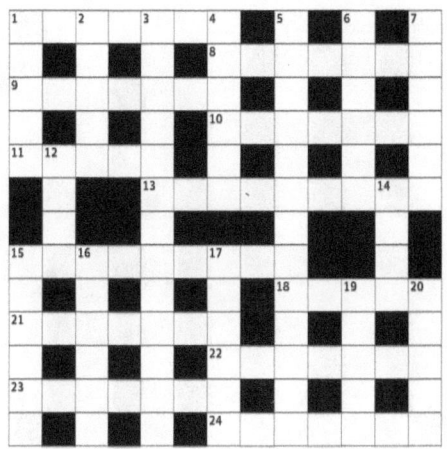

Across

1 Opportunities (7)

8 One of the variants of an element sharing an atomic number but with differing chemical properties (7)

9 Word made up of initial letters (7)

10 Own (7)

11 Register (5)

13 Appalling (9)

15 Heart chamber (9)

18 Disreputable—out of the sun (5)

21 Ship's windlass used for lifting heavy weights (7)

22 Small area off a kitchen (7)

23 Vocal vibrato—lot more (anag) (7)

24 No longer active (7)

Down

1 Fad (5)

2 Clothes-drying frame (5)

3 Big blaze (13)

4 Silly smile (6)

5 Conker tree (5,8)

6 Regain consciousness (4,2)

7 Camera attachments (6)

12 Designation—reputation (4)

14 Second-hand (4)

15 Leave (a place previously occupied) (6)

16 Sibling's son (6)

17 Large American vulture (6)

19 Following (5)

20 Bring in—give up (5)

Solution no 112

Quick crossword no 114

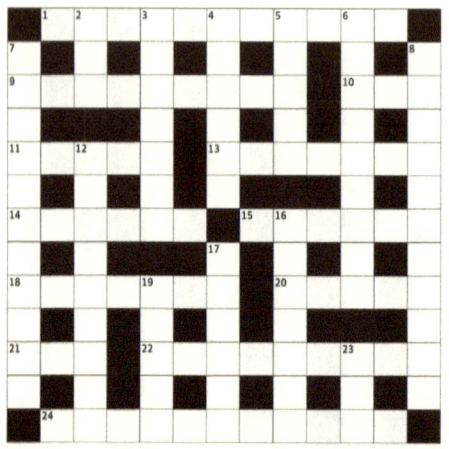

Across

1 Arizona tourist attraction (5,6)
9 Intentionally (2,7)
10 Bind (3)
11 Small and elegant (5)
13 Pharmacist (7)
14 Reflected sounds (6)
15 Enquiring (6)
18 x, y or z, possibly (7)
20 Watchful (5)
21 Rosie Lee (3)
22 Lacking life (9)
24 Found out (11)

17 To some extent (though not entirely) (2,4)
19 Sheep-like (5)
23 Period of history (3)

Down

2 Rent (3)
3 Upbringing (7)
4 Adopt a low static position—Essex river (6)
5 Female relative (5)
6 In a precarious situation (2,4,3)
7 Incomprehensible language (6,5)
8 Informal social gathering (3-8)
12 Ode to Autumn poet (4,5)
16 Lingua franca of East Africa (7)

Solution no 113

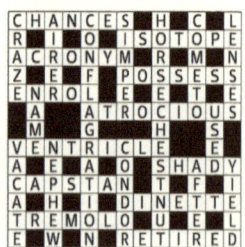

Quick crossword no 115

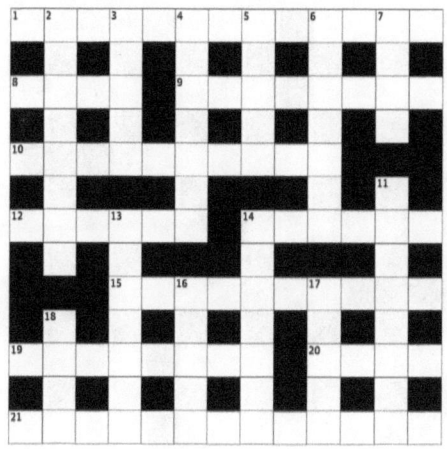

Across

1 Children's party game (7,6)
8 Thin coating (4)
9 West (8)
10 Period of enforced isolation (10)
12 Unintelligent (6)
14 Methodical procedure (6)
15 Shame claim (anag) —
29 September (10)
19 Left high and dry (8)
20 Grown-up kid (4)
21 Children's party game (4,3,6)

17 Light beer (5)
18 Festive occasion—variety of apple (4)

Down

2 Omnipresence (8)
3 Turkish seaport, formerly called Smyrna (5)
4 Embellished (7)
5 Spiny desert plants (5)
6 Formal speech (7)
7 Status—row (4)
11 Standing apart (8)
13 Self-important (7)
14 Comedian (5-2)
16 Large shell (5)

Solution no 114

Quick crossword no 116

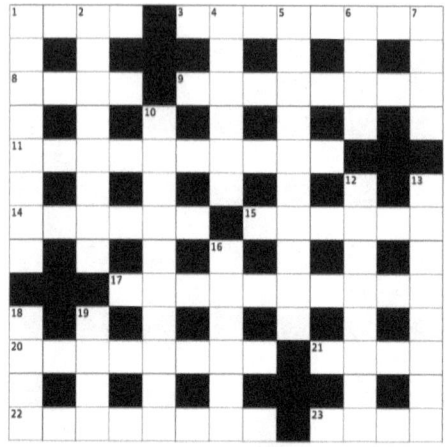

Across

1 Young male attendant (4)
3 Knitted garment (8)
8 Sesame Street character—patron saint of sailors (4)
9 Vigilante from the planet Krypton (8)
11 Puppet (10)
14 Capital of Angola (6)
15 Sick (6)
17 Trainee (10)
20 Tongue (8)
21 ___ Mitchell, Canadian singersongwriter (4)
22 Pre-Raphaelite painter and poet (8)
23 Cosy (4)

13 Dormant (8)
16 Alarming event (6)
18 Aspersion (4)
19 Objectives (4)

Down

1 Introduction (8)
2 City destroyed with Sodom (8)
4 Extortionate moneylender (6)
5 Commissioned officer (10)
6 Seductive woman (4)
7 Skating arena (4)
10 Author's pseudonym (3,2,5)
12 Large bottle (8)

Solution no 115

Quick crossword no 117

Across

1 Soon (6,4)
7 Protesting vigorously (2,2,4)
8 Not at home (4)
9 Tax—obligation (4)
10 Unauthorised absence from school (7)
12 True tobacco (anag)—basis of chocolate (5,6)
14 Clergyman's gown (7)
16 Wealthy (4)
19 Adhesive (4)
20 Become pregnant (8)
21 Contrite (10)

15 Slumber (5)
17 Mayhem (5)
18 Drawback (4)

Down

1 Creature with two feet (5)
2 Zealot (7)
3 Uncommon (4)
4 Glossy (8)
5 Large African antelope (5)
6 Part of a tea set (6)
11 Ludicrous (8)
12 Hold gently and protectively (6)
13 Cut into three parts (7)

Solution no 116

Quick crossword no 118

Across

1 Nice try, NHS (anag)—highly poisonous compound (10)
7 Card game (7)
8 Sticks (5)
10 Espied (4)
11 Non-believer (8)
13 Device for sending or receiving signals (6)
15 Occur (6)
17 Boundless (8)
18 Display (4)
21 West African country, independent since 1957 (5)
22 Ecstasy—toenail (anag) (7)
23 Nasty (10)

Down

1 Gumption—feeling (5)
2 Coarse file (4)
3 Rugged (6)
4 Patron saint of Greece (and Liverpool) (8)
5 Relentless (7)
6 Frozen water sport (3,7)

9 Renewed energy to carry on (6,4)
12 Precipitation (8)
14 Part of a song (7)
16 Greats (anag)—Italian liqueur (6)
19 Robbery (5)
20 Indonesian island—programming language (4)

Solution no 117

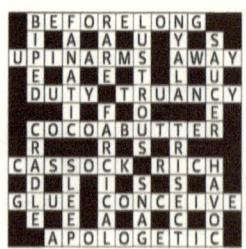

Quick crossword no 119

Across

1 Opinion sampler (8)
5 Sound of a heavy fall (4)
9 Scoundrel (5)
10 Igneous rock (7)
11 Cats in litter (anag)—woodwind player (12)
13 Bereft child (6)
14 Something unique (3-3)
17 Forever (2,10)
20 Hazel nut (7)
21 Abnormally active (5)
22 Gather a crop (4)
23 Resinous (anag)—unspecific personality disturbance (8)

8 German Protestant theologian, d. 1546 (6,6)
12 Highly desirable or alluring (2,3,3)
15 Eight-limbed cephalopod (7)
16 Soft and soothing (6)
18 Lively dance, originally from Bohemia (5)
19 Bauxite, haematite etc (4)

Down

1 After-dinner wine (4)
2 Fielding position (3,4)
3 Extra on stage as part of a crowd scene (5,7)
4 Locomotive (6)
6 Caribbean country (5)
7 Colouring substance (8)

Solution no 118

Quick crossword no 120

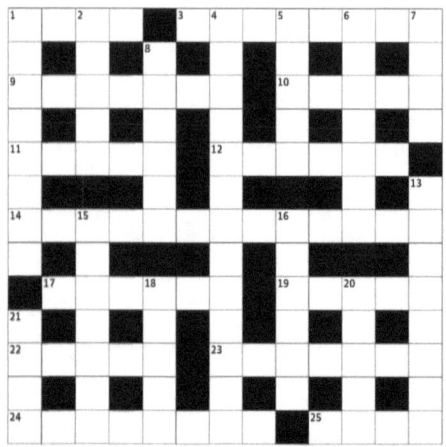

Across

1 Ridge of sand (4)
3 Cultivated plant of the genus Delphinium (8)
9 Redwood (7)
10 Braid (5)
11 Enclose snugly (5)
12 Chinwag (6)
14 Eloquent and plausible (6-7)
17 Fabric stiffener (6)
19 1941 film about a young circus elephant born with large ears (5)
22 Lloyd Webber musical (5)
23 Omitted (4,3)
24 Native American axe (8)
25 Ever so (4)

Down

1 Scatter (8)
2 Muslim women's veil (5)
4 Illegal (7,3,3)
5 Completely broken down (5)
6 Area of high level ground (7)
7 Relative speed (of progress) (4)
8 Caress (6)

13 Idolatry (anag)—with skill (8)
15 Lightest metallic element (7)
16 Fall asleep (3,3)
18 Freshwater fish (5)
20 Bond actor, Roger, d. 2017 (5)
21 First in line (4)

Solution no 119

Quick crossword no 121

Across

- **1** Improving (7,2)
- **8** Retinue (5)
- **9** Ancient wine jar (7)
- **10** Imagine (8)
- **11** Exposed (4)
- **13** Exchange for money (4,2)
- **14** List of misprints (6)
- **16** Trees (4)
- **17** Undying (8)
- **19** Not so gentle (7)
- **20** Constellation that includes Betelgeuse (5)
- **21** Migratory thrush—FA ref lied (anag) (9)

Down

- **1** Viking vessel (8)
- **2** Belisha beacon colour (6)
- **3** Little monkeys? (4)
- **4** RAF rank (5,7)
- **5** Easy progress (5,7)
- **6** Avoid (5,5,2)
- **7** Cornfield rodent (7,5)
- **12** Wood preservative (8)

- **15** Region of central Italy (6)
- **18** Having footwear (4)

Solution no 120

Quick crossword no 122

Across

1 Help (6)
4 Unit of astronomical distance (6)
8 Small jazz band (5)
9 Downright (7)
10 Student (7)
11 Lustrous fabric (5)
12 Cathedral city in West Yorkshire (9)
17 More than enough (5)
19 Libidinous (7)
21 Accumulated (7)
22 Cereal (5)
23 Slipshod (6)
24 Walk wearily (6)

Down

1 Means of approach (6)
2 One way or another (7)
3 Mar (5)
5 Performer (7)
6 Small fish (5)
7 Shedding tears (6)
9 Calm (9)
13 Lively informal party (5-2)
14 Swindle (7)

15 Long-tailed parrots of Central and South America (6)
16 Dive (6)
18 Greek philosopher (5)
20 Cane or beet? (5)

Solution no 121

Quick crossword no 123

Across

5 Overusing it (anag)—inducing
   dizziness (11)
7 Small fly that bites (4)
8 Homeless feline (5,3)
9 Collection of books (7)
11 Jewish baked roll (5)
13 Boring tool (5)
14 Writers (7)
16 Rugby halfback (5-3)
17 Enid Blyton's famous number? (4)
18 Unusually good (11)

Down

1 Be anxious—part of a fingerboard (4)
2 Artisan (anag)—My Way singer (7)
3 Young mare (5)
4 Person of great and varied learning
   (8)
5 Salad dressing (11)
6 Voyaging to other worlds (5,6)
10 Type of sweater (8)
12 Excess (7)
15 Girl's name—scarlet flower (5)
17 Sawyer's friend (from Helsinki?) (4)

Solution no 122

Quick crossword no 124

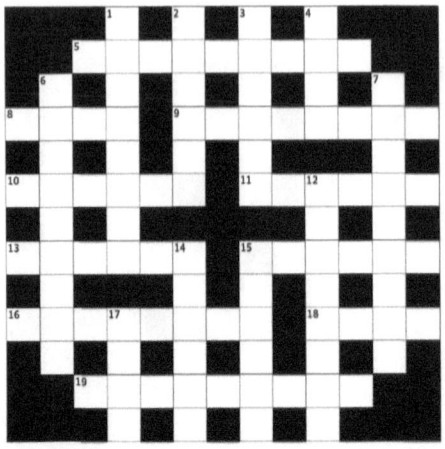

Across

5 As partial payment with the rest to come later (2,7)
8 Distinctive area (4)
9 Energetic and unpredictable person (4,4)
10 Largest island of the Dodecanese (6)
11 Young middle-class professional with a luxurious life style (6)
13 Friends in Spain (6)
15 Talkative (6)
16 Sweet-smelling (8)
18 Front—confront (4)
19 Poke one's nose in (9)

Down

1 The one expected to lose (8)
2 Weighing machine (6)
3 Group of vehicles travelling together (6)
4 Wintry precipitation (4)
6 US second-year student (9)
7 Suspension of hostilities (9)
12 Supporting structure (8)
14 Remained (6)

15 Severed (3,3)
17 Firearms (4)

Solution no 123

Quick crossword no 125

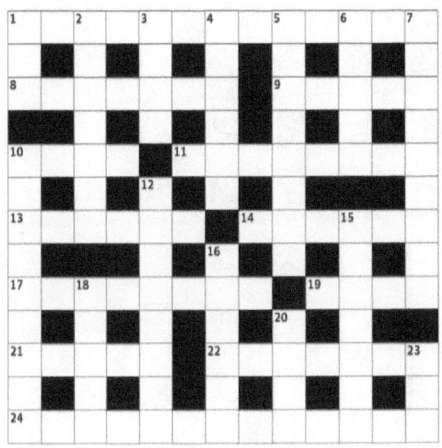

Across

1 Additional (13)
8 Signal fires (7)
9 Mountains on the boundary between Europe and Asia (5)
10 Transvestite's garb (4)
11 Disturb (8)
13 Underpants (6)
14 Means of acquiring a tan (6)
17 Lab vessel (4,4)
19 Stratagem (4)
21 Short (5)
22 Marine mammal (7)
24 Undemanding popular music (4,9)

15 Song from South Pacific (4,3)
16 Homes (6)
18 Places for pigs (5)
20 Do a runner (4)
23 Horse—badger (3)

Down

1 Weep convulsively (3)
2 Body of troops in close formation (7)
3 Get an eyeful (4)
4 Pondering (6)
5 Feeling about to vomit (8)
6 Separated (5)
7 The recent past (9)
10 Moot (9)
12 Showing appreciation (8)

Solution no 124

Quick crossword no 126

Across

1 Stopped briefly (6)
4 Demand as a right (5)
7 Chinese martial art (4,2)
8 Befitting (6)
9 Colliery (but not yours!) (4)
10 Volcano near Naples (8)
12 Uninvited guest (11)
17 Jewellery worn around the wrist (8)
19 Move by slow degrees (4)
20 Sustain (6)
21 Tilted in a particular direction (6)
22 Special delight (5)
23 In the existing circumstances (2,2,2)

13 Greek girl who unwisely challenged Athena and ended up as a spider (7)
14 Salon service (7)
15 Disease caused by vitamin D deficiency (7)
16 Take away by force (6)
18 Brilliant display—conspicuous success (5)

Down

1 Raining heavily (7)
2 Ointment (7)
3 Ambiguous (9)
4 Ionian holiday island (5)
5 Inform (7)
6 Lugubrious (6)
11 Leader of the slave revolt against Rome, 73BC (9)

Solution no 125

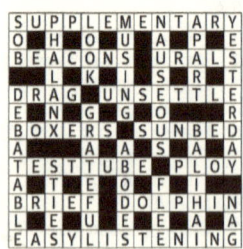

Quick crossword no 127

Across

1 Composed of viscous liquid drops (6)
4 Container for writing fluid (6)
9 Exhaust physically and/or emotionally (7)
10 Light-headed—bewildered (5)
11 Irish police officer (5)
12 Swamp (7)
13 Trans-Siberian Railway terminus (11)
18 Hissy fit (7)
20 Spokes (5)
22 Glass pane securer (5)
23 Phase of Earth's satellite (3,4)
24 Write back (6)
25 Arranged in a ring structure (6)

Down

1 Makes less clear (6)
2 Broadcasting (2,3)
3 Large hawk-like bird of prey (7)
5 Elbow (5)
6 Spanish conquistador who conquered the Incas, d. 1541 (7)
7 Vexatious (6)

8 Transfer of power to a lower level (11)
14 Syrup that may see a cough off (7)
15 Very thin (7)
16 Imagined state of perfection (6)
17 With electromechanical body parts (6)
19 (Of words) sound the same (5)
21 Spill saliva (5)

Solution no 126

Quick crossword no 128

Across

1 Pool for performing marine mammals (12)
9 Paved area outside a house (5)
10 Sharp—indicated (7)
11 Teaching both girls and boys (2-2)
12 One way of scoring at rugby (4-4)
14 Unhealthy looking (6)
15 C-F musical interval—Prince Regent George's eventual regnal number (6)
18 Lacking written authentication? (8)
20 All Blacks' war dance (4)
22 Clump of grass (7)
23 Pale brownish-yellow colour (5)
24 Plan to get out! (4,8)

Down

2 Ground grain used to make porridge (7)
3 Classical music concert for which part of the audience stands (4)
4 Communicate (6)
5 Political propaganda in art or literature (8)
6 First part of a news story (abbr) (5)
7 Confused (6-6)
8 Reusable rocket-launched craft flown by astronauts (5,7)
13 Powerful infantry weapons used against the French at Agincourt, 1415 (8)
16 Selfish and dangerous driver (4,3)
17 Plastic cup without a handle (6)
19 Cold rice balls with raw fish (5)
21 Handgun—young horse (4)

Solution no 127

Quick crossword no 129

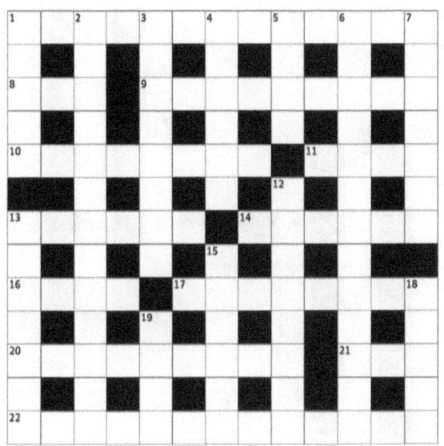

Across

1 Chinese delicacy (5,4,4)
8 Raincoat (3)
9 Seizure of the levers of power (4,5)
10 Animal in its second 12 months (8)
11 Coagulated blood from a wound (4)
13 Useful device (6)
14 In the vicinity (6)
16 Female domestic servant (4)
17 Male official with a flag (8)
20 Moving from place to place (9)
21 Male feline (3)
22 Annual US horse race for three-year-olds (8,5)

Down

1 Uneven (5)
2 Gearing that converts rotary to reciprocating motion (4-3-6)
3 Commonly designated (2-6)
4 Horse or donkey, perhaps (6)
5 Arranged neatly (4)
6 Portable boat engine (8,5)
7 Ceramic ware (7)
12 Down in the mouth (8)

13 Clever device to attract attention (7)
15 Take over by force (6)
18 Someone who objects to something being sited in their own locality (5)
19 South American country (4)

Solution no 128

Quick crossword no 130

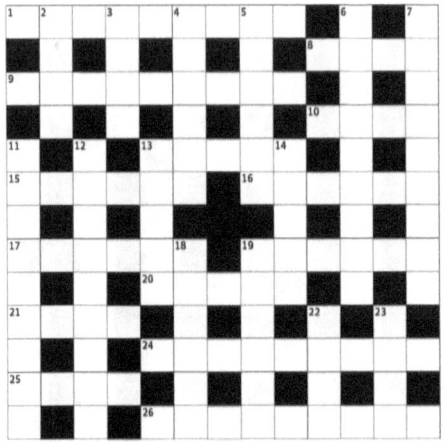

Across

1 Quip (9)
8 Sow's mate (4)
9 Silly person (with sparrow's mind?) (9)
10 Procreated (4)
13 Racist or sexist? (5)
15 Rescue (anag) (6)
16 Shellfish soup (6)
17 Strain (6)
19 Spanish wine shop (6)
20 Refuse with contempt (5)
21 Give out (4)
24 Priceless! (9)
25 Sea eagle (4)
26 Desire to travel (5,4)

Down

2 Wading bird (4)
3 Rise and fall of the sea (4)
4 Knitted jacket that buttons up the front (abbr) (6)
5 Bicycle-like device for sliding down snow slopes (3-3)
6 Nickname—Boers quit (anag) (9)

7 Path for horses (9)
11 Kind of triangle (9)
12 Arachnids with a sting in the tail (9)
13 Copper and zinc alloy (5)
14 Big hybrid of the cat family (5)
18 Run fast (6)
19 Bring up for discussion (6)
22 Lovers' row (4)
23 Fibre used for making sacking and ropes (4)

Solution no 129

Quick crossword no 131

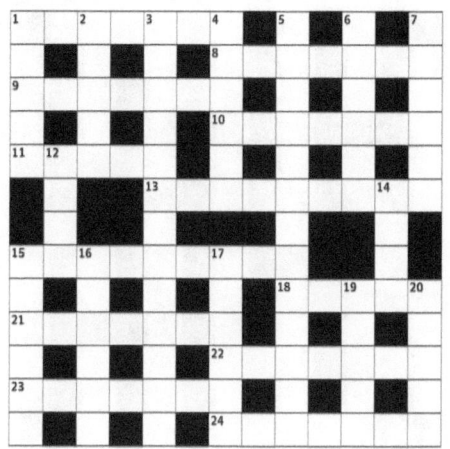

Across

1 Goes round and round (7)
8 Loss of memory (7)
9 In a quick manner (7)
10 Range of sight (7)
11 Pulls sharply (5)
13 Go ashore (9)
15 Sink liquid (9)
18 Restoration and repair of equipment etc (5)
21 Sour sticks eaten as fruit after cooking (7)
22 In a fatuous manner (7)
23 Dark underground cell (7)
24 Pickled cucumber (7)

Down

1 Given to talking too much (5)
2 Monarch's time in the job (5)
3 Humiliates (someone) (5,4,1,3)
4 Detective fiction author, d. 1957 (6)
5 Wedlock between persons from different social groups (13)
6 Respiratory problem (6)

7 Hungarian-born composer, d. 1945 (6)
12 Italian sparking wine (4)
14 Raja's wife (4)
15 Poke fun at (6)
16 Strabismus (6)
17 Cylindrical length(s) of metal, plastic etc (6)
19 Unusual and unexpected event (5)
20 Attempt to deceive (3-2)

Solution no 130

Quick crossword no 132

Across

1 California desert resort (4,7)
9 Tentative suggestions (9)
10 Precursor of the euro (3)
11 South American dance (5)
13 Delicate handling of a situation (7)
14 Street performer (6)
15 Band of warriors (6)
18 Pain—a bum log (anag) (7)
20 Canadian territory, famed for the 1897 gold rush (5)
21 Heath or Hughes? (3)
22 Charlie Parker's 'horn'? (9)
24 Rich sponge (7,4)

16 Of Summer or Winter games (7)
17 Trick player (6)
19 Side passage (5)
23 Hard durable wood of a deciduous tree (3)

Down

2 Get rid of (3)
3 Greenhouse gas produced by cows (7)
4 Rid of intrusive substances (6)
5 Author of Peer Gynt (5)
6 Supposition (9)
7 Likelihood (11)
8 Nature's perk (anag)—vessel (11)
12 TV, papers etc (4,5)

Solution no 131

Quick crossword no 133

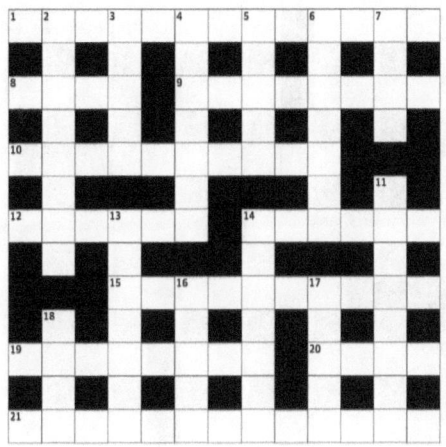

Across

1 Substance aiding the production of suds (5,8)
8 Stopper (4)
9 Loose dressing gowns—paper coverings (8)
10 French school of painting and architecture of the 1880s (3,7)
12 Passage from the mouth to the stomach (6)
14 Celtic language (6)
15 Earlier (10)
19 What may go up when the rain comes down (8)
20 Without feeling (4)
21 Large herbivorous animal native to India, Nepal, Myanmar, Borneo and Sumatra (5,8)

Down

2 Fish-viewing tank (8)
3 Encourage (3,2)
4 Fine particles from cut wood (7)
5 Snow crystal (5)
6 Marry—take on as a cause (7)
7 Spanish currency unit (4)
11 Aromatic bark used as a spice (8)
13 Africa's oldest independent country (7)
14 Trash (7)
16 Erroneous (5)
17 Guess—sit with bad posture (5)
18 Christmas (4)

Solution no 132

Quick crossword no 134

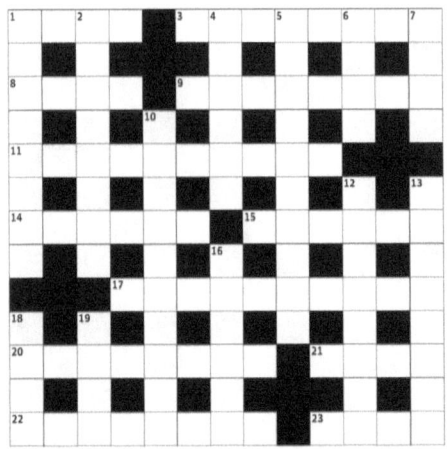

Across

1 Sound made by a dog (4)
3 Dropping of flakes (8)
8 Bound (4)
9 Duke of Marlborough's seat at Woodstock (8)
11 Affectedly genteel (5-5)
14 Distinctive uniform (6)
15 Hidden marksman (6)
17 Burly chassis for Shirley Bassey, say? (10)
20 Flat Italian bread made with olive oil (8)
21 Yugoslav marshall, prime minister and president, d. 1980 (4)
22 Wrist ornament (8)
23 Cruel and wicked person (4)

Down

1 Refuge (8)
2 Stay of execution (8)
4 Emma Hamilton's lover, who died in battle on 21 October 1805 (6)
5 Structure for testing aircraft parts by blowing air over them (4,6)
6 Again but differently (4)
7 Compact mass (4)
10 Boat that lifts out of the water at high speeds (10)
12 Organised opposition to authority (8)
13 Woodland plant with yellow flowers in spring (8)
16 Baby's sock-like shoe (6)
18 Crust over a wound (4)
19 Long involved story (4)

Solution no 133

Quick crossword no 135

Across

1 Criminal backslider (10)
7 From Honolulu? (8)
8 Ancient Greece harp (4)
9 Device for converting sound waves to an electronic signal (abbr) (4)
10 Depository for records and documents (7)
12 Line of cloud following an aeroplane (6,5)
14 Rough strong cider (7)
16 Solicit(or) (4)
19 Metallic element, Zn (4)
20 Three fourteens (5-3)
21 Pens, pencils, paper etc (10)

12 Unfortunate person (6)
13 Follower (7)
15 Full-length (5)
17 Yellowish-brown (5)
18 Three together (4)

Down

1 Royal domain (5)
2 Laugh without restraint (5,2)
3 Murder (2,2)
4 Regard with reverence (8)
5 Graceful lass (5)
6 Fawn (6)
11 Adipose tissue disappearing in adolescence (5,3)

Solution no 134

Solution no 135